Perf

Also in the *X Libris* series:

Perfect Partners

Natalie Blake

An *X Libris* Book

First published in Great Britain in 1998
by Little, Brown and Company

Copyright © Natalie Blake 1998

The moral right of the author has been asserted.

A CIP catalogue record for this book
is available from the British Library.

ISBN 0 7515 2310 0

Typeset in North Wales by
Derek Doyle & Associates, Mold, Flintshire
Printed and bound in Great Britain by
Clays Ltd, St Ives plc

X Libris
A Division of
Little, Brown and Company (UK)
Brettenham House
Lancaster Place
London WC2E 7EN

Perfect Partners

Chapter One

SUSIE JONES STEPPED out of the shower that morning with a heavy heart. It wasn't that she didn't *want* her mother to marry Jack Corcoran – Jack was a nice man and Diana deserved to be happy – but it all seemed so final, somehow, as if Diana was putting Susie's father firmly in the past.

Still, she told herself philosophically as she rubbed herself down, at least with her mother taken care of, she was free to go to London to pursue her modelling career with a clear conscience. She smiled to herself, her spirits lifting as she switched her thoughts to her own future.

Walking naked into her bedroom, she stopped in front of the full-length mirror and gazed contemplatively at herself. Her smooth, pale skin glowed pink from the shower, her hair made a darker blond by the steam. Reaching up, she smoothed it back from her face and ran a critical eye over her figure.

At five-feet-eight she was only just tall enough for the catwalk, but the photographer who had discovered her had said that wouldn't be a problem. She shivered as she remembered the way he had looked at her, and goosebumps raised up across the surface of her skin. The neat little nipples punctuating the centre of her small, pert breasts, puckered, sending a little thrill of remembered arousal down to the hidden flesh at the apex of her thighs.

Allowing her hair to fall softly on to her shoulders, Susie cupped her breasts in her hands. Watching herself in the mirror through half-closed eyes, she moved her thumbs slowly back and forth across the hard little buttons, making the heat rise beneath the surface of her skin, weakness creeping into her legs.

Without taking her eyes from her mirror image, she stepped back a few paces so that she could lean against the wall. The smooth surface of the painted plaster was cool against her heated flesh as she slid slowly down it on to the floor.

Susie sighed, eking out every second of the well-worn routine, revelling in the heightened sensations which surrounded her. The carpet felt soft against her buttocks, the air in the room warm as it caressed her skin. Her long thighs parted softly as she allowed one hand to drift down between them, stroking the downy hillock of her pubic mound with the backs of her fingers.

Her eyes caressed every inch of the image in the mirror. The sight of her own flawless body pleased her, its blossoming feminine shape turning her on far more than looking at pop stars and actors did her friends. She was beautiful – that was fact not conceit, and the act of pleasuring herself was more satisfying than anything she could imagine she might be able to do with the village boys.

She grimaced at herself in the mirror as she thought of their clumsy, inept fumblings, smiling as she wondered how they would react if they could see her now. Not with the swaggering self-confidence they all liked to fake, she guessed derisively.

2

Susie held her breath as she allowed her thighs to slide apart against the carpet. Drawing up her knees, she watched in the mirror as the pale pink jewel of her sex was revealed, just a tantalising glimpse at first, then opening, the tender inner flesh glistening with arousal, the shadowed cleft at the entrance to her body exposed . . .

Slowly, almost reverently, Susie stroked one finger along the outer edge of her labia, down one side and up the other. 'Mmmm . . .' she sighed, making herself more comfortable.

At the apex of her inner lips, a small pulse began to beat at the heart of her sex, so strong she could see it in the mirror. As soon as her clitoris slipped into view, she began to circle it with her fingertip, lightly at first, teasing it out from beneath its protective sheath, sending little shivers of pleasure radiating outward through the rest of her body.

She felt her womb contract as the pressure in her pleasure-centre began to build. The warmth spread through her legs, making her toes curl with sheer excitement, and her stomach muscles contracted as if attempting to contain the sensation. She liked to test herself, to prolong the time that she was in full control of her feelings, almost to the point of climax. It made her feel powerful, totally womanly, to control the reactions of her body, to play herself like a delicate musical instrument, the sweet notes of arousal building gradually, harmoniously towards a soaring crescendo . . .

Then, when sensation overcame her, she gladly let herself go, surrendering to it, rubbing the hard little bud of her desire harder and faster. Her reflection blurred and became indistinct as her climax spiralled through her, out of her control now, heading towards the moment of release.

When it came it was sweet, filling her with a golden warmth that seemed to encompass every part of her, making her tremble. Susie closed her eyes and threw back her head, letting out her breath on a long, blissful sigh as the sensations peaked, then began to ebb away, leaving her limp and warm and satisfied.

'Susie! Susie, are you up yet?'

The sound of her mother's voice jerked her out of her post-orgasmic languor and she jumped up, reaching for her robe.

'I've just stepped out of the shower!' she called lightly, her voice betraying nothing of her recent excitement.

'Come and have some breakfast – Rhiordan will be here in half an hour to get ready.'

Susie smiled at herself in the mirror.

'Coming!' she called and, fastening her robe, she turned towards the door.

'When you actually think about it, it's pretty disgusting, isn't it? I mean, they're getting married, so I imagine they're going to be *doing it*. Ugh!' Rhiordan gave a theatrical little shudder which made her soft, plump flesh quiver. 'This'll all be new to your mum . . . I mean, since your dad went away . . .' She trailed off, darting a glance at her friend to check she hadn't gone too far.

Susie wiped her lipstick off carefully with a moistened tissue before trying another shade. She seemed not to be aware of Rhiordan's presence, so intently was she staring at her own face in the dressing-table mirror, but Rhiordan was used to Susie's self-absorption and didn't mind. Susie was so beautiful, so *special*, it never crossed

4

Rhiordan's mind to expect anything more than the mostly one-sided friendship that had arisen between them.

'How old *is* your mother, Susie?'

Susie pursed her lips and sighed. This was the seventh lipstick she had tried, and still she couldn't quite decide which one went best with the pale pink bridesmaid's gown.

'Forty-two,' she replied absently.

'Exactly! Imagine having sex at forty-two! It must be *horrendous*!'

Susie turned to Rhiordan, a faintly quizzical look on her lovely face. 'I suppose you're right – I hadn't really thought about it.'

Undeterred by her lukewarm response, Rhiordan giggled.

'Mind you, your new stepdad's a bit of all right, isn't he? And as for that gorgeous Canadian accent – I wouldn't mind hearing that whispering sweet nothings in *my* ear!'

Susie grimaced at her own reflection, still not satisfied with the way she looked.

'Maybe you'll like his son, then,' she said absently.

Rhiordan sat on the edge of the bed and leaned forward, avid for information.

'What's his name again? Have you met him yet? How does it feel to be getting a brother?'

Susie sighed heavily, growing tired of Rhiordan's mindless chatter. Couldn't she see that she'd far rather be left alone to get ready?

'His name is Adam and he won't be my *brother*,' she said irritably, 'just Jack's son.'

'But he's going to be living here, on the farm?'

'Yes. Apparently, he's just graduated from

5

agricultural college, or whatever it is they call it out there. Jack wants him to help run the farm. But that's hardly going to affect *me*, is it, since I'm leaving for London at the end of the month?'

Rhiordan looked disappointed. If it was her mother who was marrying a handsome Canadian with an eligible son, she was sure she'd be at least a bit curious about him.

'But Susie—'

'How are you doing, girls?'

Both turned as the bedroom door opened and Susie's mother, Diana, wafted in on a cloud of *Anaïs Anaïs*. Anyone looking at Diana was left in no doubt from where her daughter had inherited her looks. Tall and slender, she looked closer to thirty than forty-two. Maturity had gently sculpted the soft edges still apparent in her daughter's face and, with her flawless skin and immaculate grooming, the result was quite stunning. Looking at her now in her flowery kaftan, with her newly styled hair and sophisticated make-up, Rhiordan thought that one could be forgiven for assuming that Diana was one of the smart metropolitan guests due at the wedding rather than a farmer's bride.

'Mummy, I can't decide which lipstick,' Susie said irritably. 'Goodness knows why I have to wear this awful dress – nothing goes with it.'

Diana smiled and picked up one of the discarded tubes of lip colour. Handing it to her daughter, she smiled at her pouting face in the mirror. In this frame of mind, her daughter looked no older than twelve.

'I admit this is hardly a fashion colour, darling, but it's so pretty on you. It's not every day that one can be bridesmaid to one's mother – couldn't you indulge me, just for today?'

6

As always, Susie's petulant mood disappeared as quickly as it had arrived. She smiled at her mother in the mirror, conscious of Diana's desire for the day to go smoothly.

Satisfied, Diana turned to Rhiordan.

'And you look lovely too, Rhiordan, dear,' she said diplomatically. 'Thank you so much for agreeing to be my bridesmaid. I think your mother is waiting for you downstairs with her camera.'

Blushing furiously, Rhiordan hurried out of the room, leaving mother and daughter alone.

'Mummy, she looks like a plump pink piglet in that dress,' Susie said bluntly.

'Don't be unkind – I thought Rhiordan was your best friend.'

Susie shrugged.

'That's why I feel I can be honest. Besides, I don't suppose we'll see much of each other once I'm living in London.'

Diana sat down, her smooth brow puckering into a frown. *When I'm living in London . . .* That seemed to be all she had heard from Susie for weeks now.

'I do wish you'd reconsider, darling. You know that Jack and I would be more than happy for you to live here while you go to university, and—'

'Mum, I am *not* going to university! I'm eighteen and I'm going to be a model. I don't want to pass up this opportunity. It's not every day that a girl gets spotted on the streets of Cardiff by a top photographer, is it?'

'No, but it worries me how little we know about this man, Susie. If I hadn't been so tied up with the wedding, I'd have gone to London myself to check him out, but—'

Susie grasped her mother's hand and gave her

fingers a squeeze. 'Please, Mummy. I know what I want and I can look after myself. I'm not a baby any more.'

Watching her daughter as she stood up and smoothed the pink satin gown over her curvy, nubile figure, Diana silently agreed, if not with the first two statements, then at least with the last.

Downstairs, there was a purposeful bustle as people went about their business. Diana and Jack were to be married in the village church, but the reception was to be held at the farm. Surveying the huge, striped marquee erected for the wedding meal, Jack Corcoran realised with a wry smile just how Diana had managed to get through such an enormous amount of money in the run-up to the wedding.

There seemed to be an entire army of caterers laying the long, linen-covered trestle-tables, working alongside two women from the local florists who were arranging armsful of flowers along the tables and stringing them across the awnings like Christmas tinsel. The local publican grinned as Jack passed, pausing for a moment in his task of rigging up a makeshift bar in the corner.

'It'll be a good night, it will, *bach*,' he said, as if the quality of the beer was the most important ingredient of the entire proceedings. Jack grinned in response and waved at Sheryl, Diana's friend, who was organising the whole shebang. Recognising the determined glint in her eye as she spotted him, Jack turned on his heel sharply. He'd had enough crisis meetings with Sheryl to know that he'd be stuck for at least half an hour if he was caught with her.

Walking outside, he glanced at his watch. Barely an hour before they were due at the church, and still Adam hadn't showed up. Why the boy hadn't taken the time to let him know his flight, he didn't know; it wasn't like him. But when he'd telephoned his ex-wife, Val, Adam's mother, she had informed him that Adam had taken himself off on a whistlestop tour of all his favourite haunts before leaving Canada.

Had he done the right thing, bringing Adam over to help him run the farm? Walking out to the meadow, treading carefully in his dress shoes, Jack squinted into the sun as he ran his eyes across Diana's acres. Peter Jones had neglected the place in the months before he left home and there would be a great deal of hard work ahead if he was to bring the farm round. Though Adam was fresh out of agricultural college, he was eager for practical experience, and Jack needed his son's help.

Of course, had he not wanted to come, he could always have refused, couldn't he? Privately, Jack was extremely pleased that Adam had answered his call for help and agreed to his request that he should be best man at his wedding. Adam had lived with Val and her dentist husband ever since the divorce ten years before, and Jack was looking forward to getting to know him properly now that he was no longer a child.

'You're looking wistful – having second thoughts?'

Jack turned at the sound of Diana's voice, his heart lifting as it always did when he saw her.

'Second thoughts? Sure – and third and fourth. And you know what?' He took her into his arms as she laughed.

'What?'

'Every one is the same as the first – I'm a lucky, lucky guy that you want me by your side at the altar.'

They kissed, oblivious to the bustle taking place a few feet away from them. As they broke apart, Jack

9

looked her up and down affectionately.

'Is this your wedding gown, honey?' he asked, eyeing the familiar kaftan with a smile.

Diana widened her eyes. 'Don't you like it?'

'I love it! But then, you could marry me in a potato sack and you'd still be beautiful.'

She laughed.

'I think I can manage something a little better than a potato sack. You wait until you see Susie. She's as pretty as a picture.'

'I'll bet. Did you get to talk to her?' he asked, regarding Diana's face shrewdly.

A cloud crossed her lovely features and he felt his heart squeeze in his chest.

'She won't listen, Jack, she's so headstrong.'

'Hmm. I wonder where she gets *that* from?' Privately, he reckoned that Susie could have done with a little firm discipline in the past; she was far too spoilt for his liking. But he was fond of her none the less, and not only because she was Diana's daughter. He recognised it was too late for discipline now. Susie was going to have to learn the hard way that the world did not revolve around her.

'It'll work out, honey,' he said now, touching the backs of his fingers lightly against Diana's face.

She smiled, turning her head slightly so that her lips brushed the backs of his knuckles, sending a deep, erotic thrill speeding through his body.

'I'm sure,' she murmured, her eyes darkening as she recognised his reaction to her kiss.

Jack was tempted to take her in his arms again, to kiss away the worry over her daughter which he could see still lingering in her eyes. But at that moment, they were hailed from the house.

10

'Telephone for you, Jack,' Sheryl called. 'It's Adam.'

Exchanging glances, Jack and Diana hurried back to the house. Diana listened anxiously to Jack's side of the conversation, raising her eyebrows questioningly as he replaced the receiver.

'He's running late, so he's going to meet us at the church,' he told her. 'What with my son and your daughter, this wedding is turning out to be far more stressful than I ever thought possible! I sure hope our kids aren't going to put the dampener on things today . . .'

Diana stepped forward and kissed him lightly at the corner of his mouth.

'They can't, my darling,' she murmured softly. 'This is *our* day and nothing is going to spoil it for us – not even our children.'

Moving into each other's arms, neither noticed Susie at the bottom of the stairs, standing very still as she watched them.

Putting down the receiver, Adam Corcoran turned back to the girl who sprawled unashamedly naked across the top of the roadside motel bed.

'Do you *have* to go?' she wheedled, her red lips forming an inviting pout.

Running his eyes lazily across her plump, white body, Adam smiled and stretched.

'Another half an hour won't make much difference,' he said, feeling himself harden in anticipation.

The girl smiled wolfishly and eased herself over to his side of the bed. Her skin felt warm and moist as she slithered against his naked body, her wide, full mouth moving teasingly across his chest. He gasped as her sharp little teeth grazed his nipples before her lips

11

moved softly, seductively down, over the taut flesh of his belly. Her tongue flickered across the surface, tracing the line of his waist, avoiding the tumescent rod of flesh that rose up from his groin, straining towards her teasing lips.

If he could remember her name, he'd beg her, but they'd met only the night before in a club where the music was too loud for conversation and the only communication they had employed was body language. He could hardly ask her name now, so Adam simply cupped his fingers around the back of her head and urged her gently to the centre of his arousal.

He gave a juddering sigh as his penis was enclosed in the soft, moist heat of her mouth. All thoughts of seeing his father again were banished from his mind, all his attention focused on the sweet, drawing sensation in his groin as the girl began to suck rhythmically on his shaft. His breath whistled softly through his teeth as her tongue sought and found the moist slit in the bulb. Burrowing gently with her tongue, she cupped his balls in one hand and squeezed.

'Jeez . . .' he murmured. Where the hell had she learned to do that? Despite the exertions of the previous evening, Adam felt as though a torrent of semen was now gathering in his balls, just waiting to explode. A fine sheen of perspiration broke out all over his body and he shivered in spite of the heat of the bedroom.

Looking down, his eyes roamed across the fleshy hills and valleys of the girl's body, revelling in the gentle undulations she made as she worked diligently at fellating him. He loved voluptuous women; abundant warm flesh he could sink into and the uninhibited approach to sex which, in his experience, such women displayed. These, to him, were far more feminine and erotic attributes than the modern idea of beauty which was portrayed as 'ideal'. Crashing bones with some stick-thin model from a fashion magazine with druggy eyes and scruffy hair could not be more of a turn off.

Reaching down, he caressed the back of the girl's neck as she began to draw him deeper into her throat. His heart began to race as he felt the moment of release approach and his hand stilled, his palm pressing gently between her shoulder-blades as the first ejaculate surged along his shaft, spurting forcefully into her willing mouth . . .

It was over much too soon, but Adam knew there was no time to linger. Conscious of time growing short, he rolled the girl over and spread her legs. Her sex was red and puffy, glistening with the dew of her arousal. Her eyes were languid, though they sparked with lambent excitement as she gazed up at him from the pillows.

'Yes . . .' she whispered thickly.

Adam dipped his head slowly, prolonging the anticipation for as long as possible. Putting out his tongue, he touched the hard little bud of her clitoris very, very gently, making her cry out. Teasing her, he flicked his tongue lightly along the outer lips of her sex, feeling the sweet coarseness of her pubic hair rasp against its surface before turning his attention to the soft, slippery folds of her inner labia.

She tasted of sea-salt and honey with the underlying tang of spilt semen from the night before. Remembering how he had plundered her welcoming body time after time, he was overcome by a rush of affection for the sensitive orifice which had welcomed him so willingly. Touching his lips against the pulsing button of her clitoris, he kissed it gently, almost reverently, causing it

13

to buck against his mouth as the first tremors of orgasm swept through her.

So sensitised was she by their coupling the night before, there was no need for him to do anything more than suck gently on the pulsating bud, tipping her over the edge into full-blown climax within seconds.

They kissed afterwards, exchanging tastes and odours that had enthralled them for hours. Both knew they would be unlikely to meet again, but there was no sense of regret or reproach. Adam was grateful, and he focused on the duties of the day, mentally leaving the small, overheated hotel room even as he dressed.

He wondered, not for the first time, if he and Jack would get on now that they were meeting as men rather than man and boy. He liked the sound of Diana, but from Jack's brief description of her, Susie sounded like a spoiled little brat. Adam liked women, adored them all, given half the chance, but selfishness and a determination to get her own way were two things which, when combined, he could not stand. And his new little sister sounded like she'd got both faults in buckets.

'Can I stay here for a bit?' the girl asked him as she watched him button his shirt.

Startled out of his thoughts by the sound of her voice, Adam grinned. 'Sure. The room's paid up until noon – be my guest.'

She stretched like a cat, unashamed of her nakedness and making no attempt to cover herself as she parted her legs. Adam caught a glimpse of fresh dew and tantalisingly pink flesh before her hand obscured his view, delving into the warm, wet folds of her flesh.

'Mmm – lovely!' she purred, making herself comfortable as she began to stroke her clitoris.

Adam laughed. 'You're insatiable!' he teased.

The girl smiled knowingly. 'Stay a little longer and test the theory!' she invited.

Adam watched as her fingers disappeared inside the deep, dark well of her sex. He swallowed and forced himself to look away. He couldn't afford to leave it any later than he already had.

'I wish I could, but I have a wedding to go to.'

'Not your own, I hope!' She looked genuinely shocked, and he laughed again.

'Not likely.'

Bending over the bed, he kissed the girl swiftly, then left. By the time he was out of the hotel he had forgotten all about her.

Susie fidgeted beside Rhiordan as they waited with Diana and the vicar outside the church door.

'We'll give him five more minutes,' the vicar said glancing at his watch discreetly.

'Thank you.' Diana strained once again to see along the narrow lane that led to the church. 'I can't think where he's got to. He phoned Jack at the house only an hour ago. I do hope he makes it – Jack will be so upset if he doesn't.'

Susie watched her mother fretting over Jack's son's absence and felt a surge of indignation on her behalf. How could he be late for his own father's wedding? As best man he should have been at the church before anyone else. Remembering what she had overheard earlier, she was gratified that she, for one, had not let her parent down.

Diana looked dazzling in her simple cream silk tube-dress, its boat-style neckline showing off the slender whiteness of her neck. Her hair was drawn up off her face in an elegant French pleat and she wore no jewellery except for the exquisite diamond stud earrings that Jack had bought her for her birthday. Her bouquet consisted of three large white lilies tied with a length of rough green florists' ribbon and held in the crook of one arm.

'You look beautiful, Mummy,' Susie said impulsively.

Diana looked surprised for a moment, then she smiled, clearly touched. 'Why, thank you, Susie,' she said emotionally, and Susie felt both embarrassed and glad that she had spoken aloud.

Just then a taxi rumbled to a halt outside the church and the wedding party all turned expectantly. A young man stepped out and poured money through the open driver's window. As he raced up the steep church path, he tucked in his shirt and ran his fingers lightly through his dark, curly hair in an attempt to tame it.

Rhiordan dug Susie in the ribs with her elbow.

'Wow!' she mouthed, her eyes widening into two round, predatory pebbles.

Susie quelled her with a frown and turned a frosty expression on her soon-to-be stepbrother as he approached. He might well be handsome in a rough, swaggering kind of way, but all she could see was an all-too-charming grin as he approached and an incorrigible twinkle in his eye.

'Diana, I presume?' he drawled in an accent far more pronounced than his father's, but no less sexy.

Before Diana could say anything, he had enveloped her in a boisterous hug which threatened to dislodge her bouquet, before delivering a resounding kiss on her cheek.

'Sorry I'm late, Ma,' he said with a grin which could only be described as cheeky. 'See you at the altar.'

Susie took a hasty step back when it looked as

though he might treat her to the same greeting. For a moment, their eyes met and Susie had the uncomfortable experience of feeling as though her mind was laid bare. Adam's lips twisted slightly, as if he knew exactly what she thought of him and didn't care in, the least. Susie felt herself grow warm, as if she had suddenly become the cynosure of all eyes. Then Adam grinned again, wiping his expression clean, leaving her wondering if she had imagined it.

Susie and Diana exchanged glances as Jack's son disappeared into the gloomy interior of the church with the relieved vicar. Diana's pale cheeks were tinged with pink and her usual composure seemed to have slipped slightly.

'Well – *he's* not quite what I expected!' was all she had time to say before the organ struck up the *Wedding March*.

Fussing with her mother's skirt as they began to make their way along the aisle, Susie silently agreed with Diana. She wasn't sure what she had expected, but she did know that Adam Corcoran was not it.

Despite the initial impression he had made, Adam performed his duties as best man impeccably, producing the ring on cue and standing straight and proud beside his father as Jack took his vows. Once the service was over and they were all standing outside in the sunshine, posing for the photographer, Susie had to admit as much, albeit somewhat grudgingly, to Rhiordan.

'You've got to admit, he is a babe,' Rhiordan whispered, watching him posing with his father.

Susie snorted. 'Not my type. But yeah, I see what you mean. Very *male*.'

She meant the last remark disparagingly, but

Rhiordan agreed with enthusiasm. It was all right for her, Susie thought irritably, she only had to look at Adam Corcoran as a new prospect, whereas she was expected to think of him as a brother. A *brother*, for heaven's sake! If she'd ever wished for one as a child, he was certainly nothing like the over-confident, boorish young man who had turned out to be Jack's son. With a little start of surprise, Susie realised she was quite disappointed.

Just then, the photographer called for the brides-maids to pose with the bride and groom and the best man. In her element, Susie smiled for the camera, confi-dent that Diana would not be disappointed with her contribution to the wedding photographs. All the while, she was conscious of Adam standing behind her, making the odd teasing remark to Rhiordan or Diana, clearly taking the whole business far more lightly than Susie thought was warranted.

She stiffened when Diana asked the photographer to take a few shots of her and Adam alone. Glancing at him, she saw the amusement in his dark brown eyes and realised he knew what she thought of him, and was laughing at her.

'A bit closer together, please – look as though you know each other, at least!' the photographer urged as Susie stood stiffly to attention.

Adam came to stand by her side and slung a casual arm around her shoulder. It was so unexpected that Susie immediately stiffened and moved away, casting him a quelling glance which clearly annoyed him. His dark brows came together in a frown and his jaw tight-ened perceptibly.

'Only trying to be friendly, sis,' he drawled sarcasti-cally.

'I am *not* your sister,' Susie hissed. 'We don't have to stand that close.'

'Well, excuse me for breathing, I'm sure!'

Susie looked away resentfully. Why was he being so boorish? He seemed to have taken an instant dislike to her ... as she had to him, she reminded herself. And certainly his behaviour now bore out her initial impression of him.

The camera whirred before she was ready – which increased Susie's ill humour – and they moved apart gratefully. Turning her head, Susie saw Adam going over to talk to Rhiordan, who was dimpling prettily at him as she gazed up adoringly through her long eyelashes. Traitor! she thought crossly as she made her way to the wedding cars.

Diana smiled at her as she approached. 'I can't wait to see the photographs, darling,' she said, reaching out to smooth Susie's hair off her forehead. 'You and Adam looked so well together. It's going to be lovely to be a real family again.'

Susie looked at her mother with horror. Surely it was only the sentiment of the day talking. Diana couldn't really think that she and Adam would ever see each other as related? That they'd ever really be family in the sense that Diana meant?

Diana looked thoughtful now, apparently unaware of what was going through her daughter's mind.

'He's quite different to how I expected him to be,' she continued, lowering her voice conspiratorially. 'He's rather handsome and charming, isn't he?'

Susie regarded her mother's flushed face incredulously. Was she the only female in the vicinity who hadn't been taken in by Adam Corcoran's questionable charm?

19

'Well, Rhiordan certainly seems to think so,' she murmured, darting her friend a pitying look.

Diana laughed. 'Give yourself time to get to know him, Susie. I'm sure you're going to be great friends.'

Susie climbed into the car without a word; she simply could not trust herself to reply.

Adam stood at the edge of the marquee and watched his father dancing with his new wife. It was good to see Jack again and Diana seemed all right, much as he had expected her to be from his occasional telephone conversations with her in the weeks leading up to the wedding. Then there was Susie.

She was still sitting at the top table, watching their parents as he had been, and toying with a glass of champagne. Adam had barely exchanged two words with his new stepsister since their clash in the churchyard, and he had the distinct impression that she was avoiding him.

If she was, he was glad of it. She was exactly as he had expected her to be: vain, haughty and self-absorbed. How on earth Jack thought they would get on well together, Adam could not explain. He had to admit, though, her vanity was not wholly unwarranted. Susie was a pretty little thing with clear, creamy skin and bright, thickly lashed eyes that, when she looked at him, provoked the most unbrotherly response . . .

'You're supposed to dance with her, you know.'

Adam looked round in surprise as a voice spoke behind him. It was the other bridesmaid, the doe-eyed, plump one he had spoken to earlier, and who had been throwing him hopeful looks ever since. Rhiordan, that was her name. He would have encouraged her, but she seemed very young.

'Excuse me?' he said now, puzzled.

'The best man always dances first with the chief bridesmaid. It's traditional.'

'Ah.' Adam glanced over at Susie, who seemed to be carefully avoiding looking in his direction, making him wonder if she was more conscious of him than she wanted him to think. 'It's Rhiordan, isn't it?' he said now.

Rhiordan blushed, pleased that he'd remembered her name. 'Yes. And you're Adam, Susie's new brother. Stepbrother, I mean,' she added hastily, afraid that he might have the same aversion to the idea as Susie had.

To her relief, Adam laughed. It was a warm, gentle laugh, and Rhiordan felt herself melt as she bathed in it.

'I have two half-sisters around Susie's age, so I have to admit, I'm a bit allergic to the idea of having a third. Besides, she doesn't seem too keen on me.'

'Oh, no, you mustn't think that! It's not you – Susie's not really keen on anybody ... I mean ... ' Rhiordan trailed off in confusion.

Adam regarded her quizzically, his head slightly on one side. 'You're her friend, aren't you?'

'Oh yes, I've known Susie since we were this high.' She moved her hand down to her knees.

And you've probably worshipped her for just as long, Adam thought shrewdly. Poor little cow.

'You know, I'd far rather dance with *you*,' he said, making Rhiordan blush from head to toe.

He noticed that she glanced quickly at Susie before accepting, and concluded that his new sister did get her own way far too often. Still, he thought philosophically as he took Rhiordan into his arms on the dance floor, Susie was going to be leaving home at the end of the month, so she was hardly going to get in his hair.

As they danced, he realised that Rhiordan was not nearly as young as she looked and, from the way she

21

pressed herself suggestively against him, not as innocent either. Her body was soft and plump and she smelled of sweet almonds. Her hair was soft and thick against his cheek and Adam had to resist the temptation to hold her closer, conscious of many curious eyes on him as he moved around the dance floor.

His father might have welcomed him with open arms, but he sensed that the locals regarded him with some suspicion, as if he was the prodigal son, as yet an unknown entity. It would take time to win their respect and to be accepted in this small Welsh village. And dancing shoulder to thigh with the young daughter of one of the villagers was not going to go in his favour. Regretfully, he eased Rhiordan into a more respectable embrace, softening his rejection with a smile.

Emboldened, Rhiordan said, 'You know, once Susie's gone to London, I'd be happy to show you around, if you like. You know, all the best pubs and stuff.'

Adam glanced at her in surprise. 'Are you old enough to go into pubs?'

'I'm eighteen!' Rhiordan replied indignantly. 'Plenty old enough!'

Adam smiled at her. He liked the way she spoke, the lilting, Pembrokeshire accent softening her words.

'Old enough?' he murmured suggestively.

Though she was still young enough to blush, Rhiordan was experienced enough to hold his eye as she replied.

'You bet.'

Adam drew her into his arms again and gave her a small hug.

'Why wait until Susie's gone away? Write down your number for me before you go and I'll call you in the week.'

She nodded against his shoulder and Adam felt his spirits lift. Susie's frigid welcome had depressed him far more than he had realised. Coming to a strange country to live with strangers, even if one of those strangers was his own father, had not been an enticing prospect, and he had hoped for some friendly company. But with Rhiordan's interest more than making up for his new stepsister's lack, he had to admit that things were definitely looking up.

Susie watched as Rhiordan and Adam moved around the dance floor. Her friend certainly hadn't lost much time, she thought cynically, but then, when it came to boys, Rhiordan always did go for what she wanted.

Anyone who knew them would probably think that she, Susie, was the experienced one, and Rhiordan, with her girlish propensity for blushing at the slightest thing, the virgin, but in fact it was the other way round. Susie had never fancied any of the boys at school and she was far too careful of her reputation, and her self-respect, to settle for second best. There were things she wanted to do, places she wanted to see before she tied herself down to a relationship and a job and all that those things entailed. While Rhiordan was looking for a husband to go with her undemanding job in the local supermarket, Susie had ambition.

And on the day that Sebastian Semple had spotted her walking along the street it had paid off, she told herself fiercely. Rhiordan and Adam faded away as she thought of Sebastian. Now, she *did* fancy *him*, she admitted almost guiltily to herself. But then he must be at least thirty, a full-grown man, with his trendy designer stubble and his sleepy bedroom eyes.

It was the eyes that had decided her. Sebastian

Semple looked at her from beneath this floppy blond fringe and his cool blue eyes seemed to see right into her heart.

'You've got what it takes to be really big, Susie,' he told her over coffee the day they met. 'Believe me, I've photographed them all – Kate, Cindy, Naomi – you name a top model and I've worked with her. And you've got that special something, just like them.'

Just thinking about it now made Susie tingle all over. She was going to get out of this little one-horse town and Sebastian was going to help her turn herself into a top model. A star.

Susie's eyes swept the room. She knew every single person there, most for as long as she could remember. In London she would know no one but Sebastian. Hastily, she pushed away the small thrill of fear that thought provoked, telling herself that Sebastian would look after her, introduce her to all the right people, take her to all the right parties. And in two, maybe three years – even sooner if she was really lucky – every person in this room would know that she had made it.

Her eyes came to rest on Adam, and she realised with a little start that he was walking towards her.

'Rhiordan tells me it's the custom over here for the best man to dance with all the bridesmaids,' he said in that infuriatingly laid-back drawl of his.

It was on the tip of Susie's tongue to refuse – she didn't want to dance with him, really didn't want to have to bother to get to know him, since she had decided on first sight that they wouldn't get on. But people were looking, smiling indulgently as the groom's son spoke with the bride's daughter, and so, reluctantly, she stood up and took his outstretched hand.

His hands were warm and dry, big enough to enclose hers completely. He smelled of lemon soap and warm skin and his hair felt soft and silky as it brushed across the top of her forehead. For one inexplicable moment as he drew her into his arms, Susie had an almost over-powering urge to move away. He was so big and well-built, so very *male*, that she felt almost threatened by him.

It was not a pleasant feeling, and Susie held herself rigid as they moved stiffly around the makeshift dance floor, waiting for the three-piece band who were play-ing to come to the end of the number so that she might reasonably escape.

Adam, however, had other ideas. As the song ended, he steered her forcefully out of the marquee and into the starry night beyond.

'What—'

'I think you and I should talk,' he said, gripping her by the elbow and marching her towards the house.

Recovering slightly from her initial shock, Susie tried to pull away, but found she was held fast.

'Let go of me!' she gasped, wrenching herself away as they reached the patio. 'What's the matter with you?'

Lit only by the lamplight spilling through the French windows of the house, Adam's features were cast in an almost devilish light.

'You're the matter, Susie,' he said tightly. 'You seem to have taken an instant dislike to me and it's upsetting my father – and your mother.'

'I don't know what you're talking about!' How dare he speak to her like this! Susie was outraged.

'Sure you do. Maybe you don't like the idea of your mother marrying again, or perhaps it's just me. To tell the truth, I don't really care what the reason might be. I can't say that you've made that great an impression on me, either. It's probably just as well you're off to London where your stuck-up attitude might be more in keeping. But our parents want us to get on, and I think we owe it to them to at least try. So cut the attitude, sis, and we'll rub along just fine.'

Susie watched, open-mouthed as he strode away from her, back towards the bright lights of the marquee. She could barely believe what he'd just said to her. He'd called her stuck-up! And he'd admitted that he didn't like her, yet he'd made it perfectly clear that he expected her to act like a loving little sister in front of their parents!

This was all too much. Adam might be all charm and affability in front of Diana and Jack, but he had let her see what he was really like.

Well, he didn't know who he was dealing with here, Susie told herself as she started back towards the marquee. How dare he assume that she didn't care as much as he did about their respective parents' feelings? She hadn't been the one who'd kept everybody waiting at the church that afternoon!

She'd put Mr High-and-Mighty Adam Corcoran right about a thing or two before she left for London. But she was even more glad now that she was going. Diana must be mad if she thought that she and Adam could live happily alongside each other on the farm! Much as she hated to destroy her mother's dream of playing happy families, Susie knew that she was going to have to disillusion her, or Jack's son would think he could take over the place. And, away from home or not, she was damned sure she wasn't going to allow that!

Chapter Two.

DIANA AND JACK sat in the small, private sitting room which led off from the master bedroom, and toasted each other with chilled champagne.

'I've barely drunk any champagne in my life before, and today I'm swimming in it!' Diana giggled as she took a sip. 'I could get used to it, though!'

Jack watched her with a small smile playing around his lips. She had changed out of the elegant wedding dress and into a new silk wrap in palest pink. He'd bought it for her some weeks before, able at once to picture her fine white, almost translucent skin glowing against the delicate colour of the silk. Although they'd agreed to delay their official honeymoon until Adam had settled in and was able to take over on the farm, Jack wanted their wedding night to be special, for Diana to *feel* special.

He did not have the words to describe the depth of the emotion he had experienced at the moment when she had pledged herself to him in church. He had waited until all their guests had departed and the children had retired before giving her the wrap, hoping that the small, intimate gift might illustrate a little of his happiness.

She fingered one lapel now, running her thumbpad across the luxurious fabric.

27

'You spoil me, Jack,' she said softly, putting her glass down on the side table at the end of the sofa. Her clear, bright eyes deepened to a pure delphinium blue as she gazed at him, reflecting the strength of her feelings. 'I'm so glad that fate brought you into my life.'

The sentiment was so close to what Jack was thinking at that moment that he felt a sudden lump rise in his throat.

'I can't tell you how much I love you, Diana,' he said quietly now. 'I never thought that, at this stage of my life, I would be starting afresh with such a lovely woman . . .'

'So it's my body you're after, is it, Jack?' She teased him, gently lightening the mood.

He smiled slowly. 'It'll do for starters,' he said, matching her tone.

Diana's eyes were very clear, very direct as she looked at him across the short distance that separated them.

'Why don't you come over here, then?' she whispered. The huskiness entering her voice did strange, wonderful things to Jack's equilibrium.

He moved slowly, slipping from his chair on to his knees, so that he was kneeling on the rug at her feet.

'I adore you,' he whispered. 'I worship you.'

Diana said nothing, just looked at him with an expression of such serenity that, for a moment, Jack was almost in awe of her. Then she reached out, her long, slender fingers tracing the line of his jaw before passing lightly across his lips, making them tremble.

'Yes, Jack,' she murmured, 'worship me.'

Leaning his forehead briefly on her knees, Jack growled softly, deep in his throat. His fingers trembled as he touched the tips against her leg, feeling the silk

28

slip against the smoothness of her skin as he pushed it aside.

Her lower legs were smooth and slender, her knees softly rounded. Raising his head and sitting back on his heels, Jack remained at her feet as he allowed his fingertips to move slowly round to the delicate skin at the back of her knee. She shivered slightly as his fingers ran across her skin and her flesh rose up momentarily in goosebumps. Glancing up, Jack saw that her expression was still composed, still serene, despite the betraying little physical signs that told him she was becoming aroused.

His own body stirred and hardened. The room seemed very quiet, as if the whole house was sleeping. Jack knew it was well past one o'clock in the morning; after the day they'd had, he and Diana would normally be exhausted. Yet he felt as fresh as he had the moment he rose that morning, as if the love and excitement which had surrounded them all day had created an energy that kept them going, seeking still more.

Diana's feet were bare, and he picked one up now, cradling the arch of her foot in his palm. She sighed as he stroked the soft skin at the top of her foot, caressing each toe in turn before bending his head so that he could press his lips into the dip where her foot met her toes. He felt the tremor travel up her leg as he darted out his tongue, swirling it between each of her toes and kissing the pearly, painted nails. Gently turning her foot in his hands, he pressed his lips more firmly against the delicate arch of her foot, stabbing his stiffened tongue against the centre and applying pressure to the spot where he knew she was most sensitive.

'Mmm . . . and the other one,' she said, managing to sound excited and commanding all at once.

29

Without a word, Jack placed her foot down on to the soft rug before turning his attention to the other foot. This time he kissed a path around the promontory of her ankle bone and up, following the sculpted line of the inside of her calf to her knee.

Bringing up his other hand, he parted her knees so that the shell-pink robe fell away to reveal the exquisite length of her thighs, and the shadowed cleft between them. Though she was still composed and passive, Jack caught the delicate scent of feminine arousal and he inhaled deeply, his face nuzzling along the silky path between her thighs.

As he reached their apex, Diana shifted slightly so that her thighs fell softly apart, allowing him access to the warm, wet centre of her. With a primitive groan, Jack sought the slippery channels of her sex with his tongue. Her thighs quivered either side of his head and he reached up to hold her still, gripping her hips with his hands and pulling her down so that he was surrounded by her femininity: taste, touch, sight and fragrance.

It was intoxicating, making him drunk with sensation, with the want of her. Diana's sex opened to him like a flower, the delicate petals of flesh retracting of their own accord to reveal the swelling bud of her clitoris, its tip shiny and hard, inviting the loving lash of his tongue. Now she cried out, her habitual composure slipping away to reveal the warm, passionate woman she was underneath – the woman who excited him to the limit of his endurance.

As soon as he felt the first wave of her orgasm rushing through the tiny bundle of nerve endings, Jack lifted his head, replacing his tongue with his fingers so that he could see her face.

He loved this: just watching her. Her cheeks were flushed with excitement, her eyes glazed and unfocused as she stared into his.

'Jack . . .' she gasped, clutching at his shoulders as her climax shook her, rendering her weak, helpless.

As she lifted her arms, the edges of her robe parted, revealing the contours of her breasts. Jack saw that her nipples were hard and shiny, her small breasts engorged and flushed. This lovely, sophisticated woman, his wife, the love of his life, was never more beautiful than at the moment of orgasm.

Unable to hold back, Jack dipped his head and drew one tumescent, aching nipple into his mouth. Conscious of her throaty moans of pleasure, he drew deeply on the teat, flicking his tongue across the surface of the puckered aureola until she cried out.

'Stop . . . oh, Jack . . . enough . . . enough!'

With a final flick at her other nipple with the tip of his tongue, Jack raised his head regretfully to find her looking at him.

'I love you,' he whispered.

Diana's eyes darkened as she whispered, 'I know. Please, darling . . . please show me how much . . .'

Jack needed no second bidding. Diana leaned back against the soft chenille cushions of the sofa and watched through half-closed eyes as he undressed. Jack was proud of his body, knew that it was fit and strong despite being almost fifty years old, and he revelled in the unashamed lust he saw glittering in Diana's eyes. That this beautiful, sexually confident woman loved him, wanted him above all others, made his heart expand in his chest, swollen with both pleasure and pride.

Released from the confines of his underwear, his cock sprang up, straight and proud. He felt his balls tighten in anticipation, a small seepage of salty moisture beading the tip of his glans as he leaned over his wife.

'Beautiful,' she whispered, reaching for him.

Her hand was cool and soft. The feel of it caressing the length of him made Jack shiver. He wouldn't be able to hold out for long if she continued to touch him, so he gently removed her hand and positioned himself between her thighs.

Holding her gaze, he sank slowly into her yielding, welcoming flesh. The ridged tube of her sex drew him inward, her warm, honeyed secretions bathing the shaft of his penis. The rippling pleasure travelled up, through his cock and into his stomach, where it created a warm glow. The heat rose, up through his chest and into his shoulders, down his arms to his fingertips. Flowing down into his thighs and calves, it warmed his feet and made the tips of his toes tingle as he wrapped her in his arms.

In slow motion, like dancers in an intricately choreographed ballet, they rolled and dropped gently to the floor. Jack felt the softness of the sheepskin rug against his naked back as Diana's body pressed against his. She levered her upper half up and leaned away from him, arching her back to deepen the penetration.

Her hair had worked itself loose from its pleat and lay softly around her face, like a white-blond cloud. The light from the single table lamp shone behind her head, so that it looked to Jack as though she had a nebula of pure golden light around her head, a halo.

'My angel,' he whispered.

He reached up to cup her breasts in his hands, rubbing his thumbs back and forth against her sensitised nipples until she groaned, half in protest, half in pleasure. He pushed her robe over her shoulders, feeling it fall in a silken mass against his thighs, and watched as she rode him, moving up and down on the slippery rod of his cock. He watched it appear and disappear between the silken-haired lips of her outer labia, feasting on the sight and sound of their love-making, feeling his own climax gathering.

The pressure mounted, making him hot and restless as he raised his hips to penetrate her further. When at last the tension was released, the ejaculate surged up his shaft, blithely defying all the rules of gravity as it exploded from him, flooding into Diana as she collapsed forward and lay full-length against him.

Flipping her over, Jack thrust into her once, twice, three times, before slumping across her, momentarily exhausted; he felt as if the energy had been sucked out of him at high speed. The heat of her body matched his and their sweat-slicked skin melded together so that it was barely possible to discern where the one ended and the other began. Jack liked the feeling. Two as one.

After a moment or two, he felt her stir beneath him, and realised he was crushing her with his weight. Lifting himself up on to his elbows, he framed her face with his hands and gazed down at her.

'My darling. . .' he whispered.

Diana moved so that he rolled to one side and slipped quietly out of her, his spent penis soft and quiescent now, curling against his thigh like a small, defenceless animal. Diana bent her head and kissed its damp tip gently. Jack cupped his hands around her face and lifted it to his. Her eyes were shining, her lips curved into a small, satisfied smile.

'Thank you, Mr Corcoran,' she said.

'My pleasure, Mrs Corcoran,' he replied, kissing her gently on the lips. 'Time for bed?' he suggested as they broke apart.

'Again?' she said with mock horror.

'To sleep, my insatiable darling,' he chided her.

Standing up, he swept her up into his arms and carried her, laughing happily, into the bedroom.

At six the next morning, Susie saddled up her horse, Ginger, and headed off into the surrounding countryside. Despite the early hour, the air was refreshingly cool rather than cold against her face. As she left the grounds of the house, she turned into a field and gave Ginger his head.

She had been too wound up to sleep much the night before, what with the excitement of the wedding and the frustration of meeting Adam for the first time, but she didn't feel in the least bit tired as she cantered across the open ground towards the woodland which bordered their land. Riding always invigorated her, and it was one thing she knew she would miss in the city.

Not the only thing, of course, she reminded herself hastily. She would miss her mother, even Jack, and Ginger probably most of all. But she didn't think she would particularly miss her friends. They were all scattered now anyway, having completed their A levels and gone on to jobs or college courses.

Passing beneath the trees, Susie headed for the glade where she habitually rested and watered her horse before deciding how much farther she wanted to ride. The canter had left her hot and sweaty and she allowed Ginger to take his time picking along the narrow bridlepath through the woods.

To reach the glade, she had to climb up the steep, wooded hillside and breach the brow. Ginger took the tortuous, but familiar route in his stride, ambling down the hillside along the zigzagging pathway. Towards the bottom, the woodland opened out on to a circular, grassy area, transversed by a narrow, winding stream.

It wasn't until she had broken through the trees and was almost on top of him that she saw someone had beaten her to it. Jack's horse was cropping the grass lazily by its rider, who had dismounted and was crouching by the stream, bringing up the cool, clear water in his cupped hands and splashing it on to his face, much as she had intended to do herself.

'You!' she cried, recognising Adam.

As he stood up, Susie realised that he was as surprised to see her as she had been him, though he recovered himself far more quickly.

'Good morning,' he said, treating her to his wide, face-splitting grin. 'I didn't have you button-holed as an early riser.'

Susie immediately bristled, wondering what he meant.

'I often ride first thing in the morning,' she said stiffly. 'It's my favourite time of day.'

'Mine too. Hardly anyone up and the whole world looking shiny and new.'

Susie glanced at him in surprise. Dismounting, she joined him by the side of the stream, her curiosity over-coming her pique that he had found and appropriated her favourite spot.

'I don't normally see anyone round here,' she commented.

Adam laughed ruefully. 'Sorry.'

'Oh, I didn't mean—'

'Sure. Back home you can ride for miles without ever seeing another living soul.'

'Are you going to miss it?' Susie asked him curiously.

Adam shrugged, his dark eyes roaming the sun-speckled glade thoughtfully.

'I guess. But Canada's not going anywhere anyhow, so if I ever want to go back. . .' He left the sentence hanging in the air and, as if by unspoken mutual consent, they began to walk alongside the stream, leaving their horses grazing contentedly.

In the early morning sunshine, dressed in corduroys and a battered wax jacket, Adam seemed quieter, softer, altogether less abrasive than the man Susie had met at the wedding. The transformation confused her, catching her off guard.

'Do you think you will? Go back to Canada, I mean?' she asked him after a few minutes.

He slanted her a grin.

'Not as soon as you might hope, sis,' he said, instantly sounding much more like the Adam to whom she had taken an instant dislike the day before.

'Don't call me that,' she snapped, annoyed with him for reigniting her irritation.

'Why not?'

He seemed genuinely puzzled by her reaction, and Susie took a deep breath, wanting to hang on to the fragile sense of connection she had felt with him only moments before.

'Because . . . because it makes me sound about twelve years old!' she said after a moment.

Adam laughed. 'Really? Still, you're not far off that, are you?'

Realising he was teasing her, Susie did not deign to reply. They had been walking for a few minutes, heading for the edge of the woodland. As they reached the point at which the entire valley lay spread out before them, Adam gave a low whistle.

'Would you look at that!' he said, clearly surprised.

'It's beautiful, isn't it?' she agreed, looking out across the lush, rolling farmland towards the distant Preseli Hills silhouetted against the skyline in the distance. 'All the land to the left of us belongs to the family. Our farm curves round below the woodland and out behind us, back towards the house.'

'I hadn't realised it was quite so big. Jack is going to give me the guided tour later today, but I guess it'll be a while before the lovebirds emerge.'

Susie felt a little uncomfortable at her mother being referred to as a 'lovebird' and changed the subject.

'We used to own the right-hand side too, but my father sold it off piece by piece in the years before he left.'

She felt Adam's curious eyes on her, but he didn't say anything and she was grateful. The last thing she wanted was to have to explain the actions of a father she hadn't seen since she was six years old.

'It must have been tough for Diana running things on her own for the past twelve years,' was all he said.

'I suppose. But Mummy's tougher than she looks and, of course, she's had Jack to help her for the past two.'

They stood in a silence that was almost companionable for a few moments, each wrapped up in their own thoughts while drinking in the panorama spread out before them. The early morning mist was beginning to lift now, the sun growing stronger. The sound of sheep calling carried on the light breeze and the drone of a tractor reached them from somewhere in the distance.

There was no traffic on the narrow road that bordered their land, and no sign of human life except themselves.

'How can you bear to leave?' Adam said after a while.

Susie looked at him in surprise. 'It's all very well as a view, but there's nothing to do here at all.'

Adam turned to her with an expression of mild enquiry on his face. 'Oh? And what is it you want to do so badly, Susie?'

She made an impatient gesture with her hands.

'You know . . . I want to meet new people, see new places, try new things. I want to *live*. That's all.'

'And you think you can do that more easily in the noise and grime of London?'

'Yes.' She cast him a defiant glance, deliberately turning her back on the tranquil view of the valley and setting off back the way they had come. 'I'm going to be a top model someday, and I can't make my dreams come true if I stay in this hole-in-the-wall village. You know, everyone knows everyone else's business, and everybody has an opinion about everything you say and do. Don't you think you'll feel buried alive in a small place like this?' she challenged him as he caught up with her.

'No.'

'It's not always as pretty as this, you know. Once the winter sets in, everything's under snow and you're cut off at the farmhouse with no one for company except your family. You won't think it's so quaint and picturesque then. Don't you think you might even get bored?'

'No.'

'You sound very sure.'

He shrugged, running his fingers through his hair as

if wanting to feel the warming air against his scalp.

'If it's excitement you want, you can find it wherever you are. You've got friends, haven't you? After all, you've lived here all your life.'

Susie made a face. 'That's exactly the point. I've known all these people forever, and I'm bored with them just as I'm bored with Wales. I deserve better than this, and I'm going to go out there and get it. Sometimes you have to grasp the nettle and move on in life. That's what you've done, isn't it? You've left all your old friends behind to come over here.'

'That's different.'

'How?'

Adam glanced at her, his expression unreadable.

'I've not turned my back on my old friends, making them feel they're not good enough any more.'

'Nor have I!'

'You should listen to yourself. Thinking you're better than everyone else, that you deserve more.'

'You're deliberately twisting what I say to make me sound like a stuck-up little brat,' Susie complained angrily. 'Is that really what you think of me?'

Adam clicked his tongue at Jack's horse, holding out his hand to grab the reins as the animal responded and approached.

'All I'm saying is that you can't get whatever it is you're looking for by turning your back on where you came from. People aren't disposable.Your friends and relations are part of who you are.'

'And you're an expert at gathering the right people around you to give you what you need, I suppose?'

Adam sighed. 'You don't need other people to give you what you need – you've got to find that inside yourself.'

39

Susie laughed. 'Is that right? And where do you get this inexhaustible supply of happy experiences from?'

'I get it from in here,' he said, tapping his forefinger against the side of his head. 'I have all I need in my head and my heart – I don't need to prove anything to anybody.'

'Nor do I!' Susie said crossly, mounting up and following him out of the glade.

'So that's why you're off to seek your fortune in the big city, is it? Because you have nothing to prove?'

'You think you've got it all worked out, don't you, Adam-Smartarse-Corcoran? Yet you don't know the first thing about me.'

He turned in his saddle and looked at her. The lazy smile had gone now and there was no warmth in his eyes.

'Let's face it, honey – what is there to know?'

'What? Who the hell do you think you are, speaking to me like that?'

To her horror, Susie felt hot tears spring to her eyes. For a few minutes there, she had actually thought she might get to like this new stepbrother of hers, and she resented him bitterly for ruining the illusion.

Adam shook his head.

'I know who *I* am, little sis. And when you grow up, hopefully you'll know who you are too.' He urged his mount forward, moving away from Susie so that she was left staring after him, simmering with indignation.

'I'm not your sister!' she yelled at his retreating back.

There was a phone message from Rhiordan waiting for Adam back at the house. He didn't feel like speaking to anyone; he was angry with himself for getting embroiled in another verbal scrummage with Susie, and

40

angry with her for reinforcing his initial impression of her. It would make life so much easier if they liked one another and could get along.

'Morning, Adam – been out for a ride?'

He turned to find Jack meandering down the stairs in his dressing gown. He grinned. 'Just surveying the acres,' he teased, making an effort to put his ill temper behind him. 'Heavy night?'

'Don't be so cheeky! What's that?' Jack asked, nodding at the piece of paper in Adam's hand on which he had jotted Rhiordan's phone number.

'Just a number.'

'Cutting a swathe through the local talent already?'

'Hardly – it's Rhiordan's. You know, the bridesmaid?'

Jack gave him a look. 'Nice enough girl, but watch your step there, son; the mother's a bit of a dragon.'

Adam laughed. 'You don't need to worry about me,' he assured his father as they made for the kitchen. 'Mothers are a speciality of mine.'

Jack said nothing as he made fresh coffee and poured it into three fine china mugs. The pungent scent of coffee beans filled the large, sunlit room.

'Have you seen Susie? Is she up yet this morning?'

Adam snorted loudly, without thinking.

'Sure, I've seen Susie. We kind of bumped into each other earlier, while out riding.'

'How are you getting along?' Jack asked cautiously.

Adam gave him a speaking glance. 'How did you expect that we would get on?' he countered.

Jack sighed and sat down at the scrubbed deal table opposite his son.

'You know, Adam, Susie's not a bad girl, she's just a little headstrong.'

'You can say that again!'

41

'And she's used to getting her own way over things. I should imagine she feels a little bit put out over you coming to live at the farm. Wouldn't you be, in her position?'

Adam shrugged. 'Maybe. But then she's leaving pretty soon, or so she keeps telling me.'

'That's another thing – Diana isn't at all happy about Susie's plans, and I have to admit, neither am I. We had hoped that if you two got along, maybe you might persuade her to have a rethink. She might listen to you.'

'You're kidding!' Adam was incredulous that such an idea had even crossed his father's mind. He and Diana must be so wrapped up in each other that they'd lost all sense of reason as far as their respective children were concerned.

'Not really, Adam. And, that aside, we had hoped that you'd both make some effort to get along anyway. It would mean a lot to Diana and me.'

He stood up and, picking up two mugs of coffee, smiled at Adam. 'Susie's not the easiest girl in the world to live with, but she's a good girl at heart. Think about it, son, that's all I ask. Okay?'

'Sure. I'll do my best – but it takes two, y'know?'

Jack's laugh was humourless. 'She'll come round. Try using some of the famous Corcoran charm you seem so proud of on her,' he said as he walked out of the door.

Adam stared after him, wondering if Jack really believed his own words. He made getting along with Susie sound easy, while in reality Adam couldn't see that they'd got anything in common at all. All that rubbish about making it big in the city. He'd bet his last dollar that Susie Jones had a shock coming to her when her fantasies met reality.

The thought made him frown. He could understand

why Diana was worried about her. For all her loud talk, there was an innocence about Susie that was quite alarming. And London was a long, long way away from the safety of her home and family . . .

A movement in the fields beyond the house caught his eye and he turned to see Susie heading for the stables. No doubt she was all stirred up after their run-in earlier, maybe even hoping for a replay. If that was the case, she was going to be disappointed, he thought grimly.

He felt annoyed with himself for allowing the niggle of worry to enter his head. Susie was not his responsibility; he didn't want the complication of caring about her. On an impulse, he picked up his coat and made for the door.

He'd head for the village and ring Rhiordan from a payphone. It didn't look as though Jack was in any hurry to start the day, and the thought of being cooped up with Susie all morning did not appeal. At least Rhiordan would be congenial company.

With his mind made up, Adam set off and was half a mile down the lane before Susie made it through the back door.

Chapter Three

DIANA CAME DOWNSTAIRS to find Susie wandering restlessly about the house. That morning's scene with Adam had upset her and she couldn't seem to get it out of her mind. Though she knew he had no right to walk into their lives and criticise her, the picture he had painted of her made her feel uneasy. It was like looking into a fairground mirror and not liking what she saw, even though she knew it was a distortion of reality.

'What's the matter, darling?'

She turned at the sound of her mother's voice. Diana looked radiant in a pale pink silk robe Susie had never seen before. A present from Jack, no doubt. Happiness seemed to radiate from her every pore and she carried with her an aura of deep, sensual contentment which made Susie feel inexplicably uncomfortable. Somehow, Diana's serenity seemed to exacerbate her own restlessness and she had to make an effort to smile.

'Nothing. Where's Jack?'

'He's taken the tractor down to the south field.' Diana smiled ruefully and shrugged her slender shoulders. 'Honeymoon or not, life goes on.'

Privately, Susie thought that if she ever married, it would not be to a man who put his work before her. Her husband would have to adore her, make her the most important thing in his life. She had no intention of becoming a farmer's wife, that was for sure. A brief image of London and the life that awaited her there flashed through her mind, making her smile.

'That's better!' Diana said, mistaking the reason for her change of expression. 'You were looking quite glum.'

Susie veiled her expression and smiled. 'Shall I make you some breakfast?' she asked guilelessly.

'Toast would be nice – but only if you join me.'

'I'm not very hungry,' Susie protested as they walked through to the kitchen together.

'Have you had breakfast?'

'No – but then it is nearly lunchtime. I'll eat then.'

'You'll eat now,' Diana said firmly, 'and if you don't show signs of eating properly between now and the day you leave, you'll not be going to live away from home at all. Do I make myself quite clear, Susie?'

'Oh Mummy, do stop trying to be stern and sit down,' Susie said, giving her mother a brief hug. 'It doesn't suit you. I'll eat toast with you if it'll make you happy. It's no big deal.'

Diana watched as Susie moved around the kitchen, her eyes roaming her daughter's slender figure in the tight-fitting jodhpurs and figure-hugging T-shirt. The girl didn't have much flesh on her bones. It wouldn't take many weeks of eating badly to turn her slenderness into a worrying thinness.

There seemed to be no getting through to Susie that she must be aware of such things and take care of herself. Diana worried absently at a hangnail with her teeth, as her daughter prepared their breakfast.

'How are you getting along with Adam?' she asked when Susie was sitting opposite her at the scrubbed deal table. 'Jack said you went riding together this morning.'

Susie nearly choked on the piece of toast she had been nibbling. Such information could only have come from Adam and she could barely credit his cheek. Just what did he think he was playing at, giving Diana the impression they had been out riding *together*? She had no objection to being civil in front of the parents, but no way did she want to give them the idea that she and Adam had suddenly hit it off and were ready and willing to play happy families after all that had been said.

'We bumped into each other, yes,' she admitted guardedly.

Diana smiled happily, apparently oblivious to her daughter's unease. Or choosing to ignore it, Susie thought cynically, which, knowing Diana's hopes for the future, was far more likely.

'He's awfully handsome, isn't he?'

Susie shrugged.

'I suppose some might think so. All that dark, curly hair and those brooding brown eyes. Personally, I prefer blonds.'

'I see. Is Sebastian blond, by any chance?'

'He is actually. And blue-eyed.' Susie smiled. 'Sebastian has the kind of eyes that seem to see right through you, as if, when you're talking to him, you're the one person in the whole world he wants to listen to. And he has the most beautiful voice; sort of deep and silky and well modulated without being too plummy. I could listen to his voice all day . . .'

Watching Susie's face as she talked, Diana wondered if she realised how revealing her expression was. She arranged her own features carefully to hide her dismay. This situation was even worse than she had thought –

Susie was obviously infatuated with the photographer. Goodness knew what line he'd fed her when he'd 'spotted' her on the streets of Cardiff.

'You know, darling, Jack and I would feel much happier if we could meet this Sebastian before you leave for London with him,' she said carefully.

Susie smiled happily. 'Of course. Sebastian said you'd want to check things out; most parents do.'

'Really?' Diana felt as if the wind had been taken out of her sails, reducing her objections to nothing.

'Yes. He's going to ring me before I go, to arrange to come and see you. But really, Mummy, you are going to have to learn to trust me, you know.'

Reaching across the table, Susie touched her mother's hand. Diana caught hold of her fingers and squeezed them. Either Susie was incredibly, worryingly naïve, or Sebastian Semple really was the genuine article.

'Darling, I do trust you. I just—'

'Don't want to let go. I know. And I'll miss you too, when I've gone. But I'll come home between jobs and you can come up and visit me once I'm settled somewhere. We could go shopping, maybe take in a show . . . It'll be fun.'

'That's another thing – surely you'd like me to help you find a flat?'

'It's not necessary. Sebastian is arranging all of that. He has loads of contacts and stuff. Besides, you've got enough to do here now that Jack and Adam are about to reorganise everything. You don't want to have to bother with coming to London and flat-hunting.'

'It wouldn't be a bother, dear,' Diana murmured, watching as Susie cleared away the plates and stacked them in the dishwasher ready for Mrs Evans to deal with later.

Was that a note of bitterness she had detected in the younger girl's voice when she had mentioned Jack's plans for the farm? She'd never discussed the business side of things with Susie and it had not occurred to her before that she might resent the way the last traces of her father were being swept aside by her mother's new husband.

Diana felt a cold chill tickle her spine as it struck her that this could be the reason why Susie had leapt at the chance to leave home when the opportunity presented itself. Yet she had always seemed genuinely to like Jack; it was only Adam's arrival which seemed to have caused a problem. She should have talked all this through with Susie; she couldn't bear the thought that her daughter might feel driven out of her own home . . .

'Susie—'

The telephone rang and Susie picked it up. Her expression softened and she turned her back to Diana as she spoke into the receiver. Diana didn't need to be told who was on the line and the little worm of unease that had been burrowing in the pit of her stomach squirmed.

'It's Sebastian,' Susie said unnecessarily, covering the mouthpiece with her hand as she turned back to her mother. 'Can we invite him for dinner on Friday evening?'

Diana nodded.

'Ask him if he would like to stay the night,' she said. 'It's a long way to travel just for dinner.'

Susie relayed the invitation and blew Diana a kiss as it was accepted before turning her attention back to the telephone.

Diana decided on a discreet exit. As she made her way upstairs to the shower, her mind replayed their conversation. She didn't feel any easier with the repetition, but at least she now knew she would get to meet Sebastian. The fact that he had offered to come to the house and meet Susie's family ought to reassure her that he wasn't the charlatan she realised now she had him pegged for. Yet somehow Diana could not allow herself to relax and be reassured.

Rhiordan glanced sideways at Adam through her lashes. They were walking through Bowen's Wood, to the east of the village. Though the sun was warm, a cool breeze blew through Adam's hair, lifting it away from his scalp. In profile, his face was strong and lean, his nose narrow and slightly hooked, his cheekbones like two delicately sculpted wings on either side. He was taller than her by at least six inches, and broad enough to make her feel small and feminine beside him.

He carried easily in one hand the picnic hamper she had hastily prepared when he had called, the muscles in his arm rippling slightly as he swung the basket in time with each step.

She hadn't expected him to return her call so quickly, but she was glad he had. She liked what she had seen so far of Adam Corcoran, and the fact that he was here with her now showed he was interested in her too. Though she had to admit, he had seemed rather distracted ever since he had arrived, as if he was here in body, but his mind was far away from her.

'So, what do you think of the place so far?' she asked him now. 'Do you think you're going to like it here?'

Adam started slightly, as if suddenly remembering he was not alone. For an instant, Rhiordan felt piqued; then he smiled at her, and her stomach fluttered with delight.

'I like it here already – beautiful countryside, family,

49

friendly people . . .' His smile became more seductive, more intimate. 'What more could any man want?'

Was it her imagination, or had his voice taken on a thrilling little *frisson* of sensual promise? Rhiordan dimpled at him, but allowed her eyes to slide away. She didn't want him to think she was too obvious. At least, not until she had satisfied herself of one little thing . . .

'And how are things at the farmhouse? Has Susie come round yet?' she asked, contriving to be casual.

Adam snorted. 'Is there any likelihood of that, do you think?'

Rhiordan hid her relief by lowering her eyes. Things could have been awkward if Susie had decided she liked her new 'brother' after all.

'Probably not. When Susie makes up her mind about something, she can be pretty stubborn. Is that why you're here – to get away from Susie?'

They had reached the narrow track that meandered through the woods to the meadow beyond. The sunlight glittered through the canopy of branches above their heads, patterning their faces and bare arms with lozenges of gold. Rhiordan could feel herself holding her breath as she waited for his reply.

Adam stopped walking. Surprised, Rhiordan turned to him, swallowing convulsively as she recognised the expression in his eyes.

'I'm here because you invited me,' he reminded her.

The words were simple, but the weight of meaning behind them was far more complex. Rhiordan felt as though she had lost the use of her legs as she allowed herself to be mesmerised by the naked flame of lust she could see in Adam's gold-brown eyes. Knowing that her own eyes were glowing with an equal fire, Rhiordan gave up trying to be coy and allowed her true feelings to show.

'I know a lovely spot farther into the wood,' she said, aware that her voice had grown husky, deepening to betray her desire. 'The grass is as soft as thistledown and the trees are spaced farther apart than they are here, so the sun can shine through . . .'

Adam held out his hand.

'Lead on,' he said, his warm fingers curling around hers as they resumed walking.

They did not speak again, tramping through the wood in a silence pregnant with expectation, desire lending wings to their feet. Rhiordan felt the sweet, heavy pulse of arousal beating time with her heart and walked faster, leading Adam along by the hand towards the glade that was her favourite trysting spot.

'Wow!'

Adam put down the wicker hamper and stood for a moment, looking around the clearing, taking in the lush, verdant grass edged by wild toadstools growing in a haphazard ring, skirting the base of the trees. Above them, the sky arced in a deep, sapphire brushstroke, unmarred by a single cloud. There was no sound save that made by the birds and the industrious buzz of the bees as they flitted amongst the wildflowers.

'It's an enchanted place,' Rhiordan told him, dancing into the middle of the fairy ring. 'A place for magic.'

Adam's eyes darkened as he watched her, his senses heightened by the beauty of the place. With her dark hair flying free and her cotton dress clinging to the generous curves of her body, he fancied she looked like a wood nymph: a voluptuous, sensual deva, sent by the gods to enthral him.

Declaring himself a willing victim, he stripped off his shirt, delighting in the kiss of the sun against his naked skin. Casting it aside, he lifted up his arms and turned

51

his face to the sun. The breeze rippled across his flesh, making it rise in goosebumps, not through cold but through sheer pleasure.

Rhiordan laughed happily. 'Now the trousers – you have to take off the trousers! Clothes are an insult to the fairy folk!'

'Go on, then,' he replied. 'If my pants are coming off, I don't see why you should keep your dress on.'

'You first,' she insisted, watching him with eyes that seemed to devour him.

Adam laughed. Rhiordan's greedy, uncomplicated lust was refreshing, not to mention arousing. He felt himself relax, the edgy tension from his encounter with Susie flowing easily away.

Rhiordan watched as Adam unfastened his belt and pulled it slowly through the loops of his trousers. His bare torso glinted in the late morning sun, his skin smooth and shiny, like newly unwrapped caramel toffee. Rhiordan felt her mouth water. She would like to lick that flawless skin, trace the line of his chest and belly with her tongue until she reached the manicured line of fine hair which she could see now, arrowing down towards the waistband of his boxer shorts . . .

As his trousers skimmed down the length of his strong, lightly furred legs, Adam shucked off his socks so that when he straightened, he was naked save for the pure white fitted boxers. Rhiordan's eyes followed the line of his semi-erect penis and he felt it engorge and swell under the heat of her gaze.

Raising her eyes slowly to his, she gave him a small, mischievous smile. 'I needn't have brought the picnic,' she said, as her fingers toyed provocatively with the top button of her dress.

Adam felt his throat tighten as she slipped the

button slowly through the buttonhole, revealing a tantalising glimpse of plump white cleavage. When he had met her the day before, he had thought she was very young, but he realised now that it was simply the unflattering bridesmaid's dress that had made her seem so. To judge by the speculative gleam in her eye as she watched him watching her, she certainly wasn't inexperienced.

Rhiordan saw Adam's hungry look and felt a surge of power. Nothing beat this, nothing else could give her the high she got when she had a man in the palm of her hand like she had this one. This was when she knew without a doubt that the female was the stronger sex, and she revelled in being a woman. She might be not quite nineteen, but she had been an eager pupil, learning quickly how to manipulate her lovers so that they were ready to do anything for her ... anything she wanted.

'We-ell,' she said now, pouting provocatively, 'I wonder if you're going to make this worth my while? Not like that, silly,' she said, laughing as she saw from his startled expression that he had misinterpreted what she meant. 'I don't want *paying* ... well, not in money, anyway ...'

Adam's relief was almost comical, his discomfort at the possibility of having offended her quite touching.

'What is it you *do* want, Rhiordan?' he asked, his low voice slipping over her sensitised nerve-endings like a lover's caress.

She slipped another button through its buttonhole before replying. 'Just you,' she said with a wicked giggle, '*all* of you.'

Adam moved towards her slowly. The grass was unusually silky beneath his feet, long enough to tickle his calves as it brushed against his naked flesh. He imagined how it would feel to lie unclothed upon the springy blanket of grass, and shivered involuntarily.

'Stay where you are,' Rhiordan said, holding up her hand to stop his approach. 'We have plenty of time. And I want this to last a long, *long* time.'

Adam opened his mouth to say that he wasn't sure he could hold out that long, but something in her expression stopped him. This was a game to Rhiordan, and from the way that his cock was pressing firmly against the Lycra support of his boxers, Adam knew his body was more than happy to play along with her.

Sinking into the long grass, he made himself comfortable and allowed her to set the pace.

Rhiordan took her time with the rest of her buttons, caressing each smooth ball before pressing it through the buttonhole, with a soft 'pop'. She could feel Adam's eyes caressing the sliver of flesh exposed at the opening, more warming than the sunshine which beat down from its zenith above them.

Her breasts felt heavy and full, the nipples taut with arousal. Between her legs, the purse of her sex had softened and swelled, ripening like a soft, juicy fruit, her outer lips waiting to be peeled away to reveal the moist, succulent centre of her.

She moaned softly as she imagined Adam's fingers pressing into her, his hot tongue searching for the hard little pip at the core of her. Slowly, she peeled away the front of her dress to reveal her nakedness beneath. The sharp intake of breath as Adam saw she was not wearing any underwear was clearly involuntary, and the sound of it sent a thrill rushing through her.

All the way along the path she had hugged this little secret to herself, delighting in the fact that, though he knew she wanted him, he hadn't realised she was ready for him. Prepared.

The dress slipped softly over her shoulders and fell to the ground in a silky heap. Totally naked, Rhiordan held Adam's eyes as she raised her arms to the sky and slowly, gracefully, pirouetted on her toes.

'You're beautiful,' he breathed, entranced by her lack of inhibition. 'Like an ancient fertility goddess.'

Rhiordan held out her arms. 'Come and worship me, then, mortal,' she said, laughing.

Adam rose and made to move into her arms. He stopped as Rhiordan held up her hand.

'Uh-uh, not so fast!' she said.

Adam stared at her. The pupils of her eyes had dilated so much that they covered the iris, making her eyes two deep, black, fathomless pools. If the eyes are the windows of the soul, he thought suddenly, he was fascinated by what he saw in Rhiordan's.

Mesmerised, Adam waited expectantly, aware that what had started out as an uncomplicated romp was fast turning into something darker, more erotic. Rhiordan smiled as she recognised the dawning realisation in his eyes and beckoned him forward. He enfolded her in his arms without hesitation, a small, involuntary growl of satisfaction rumbling in his throat.

Her body was soft and pliant, her flesh firm but abundant, and scented with roses. He ran his fingers through the luxuriant fall of her thick, dark hair and raised her face to his.

Her eyes were shining with a luminosity that extended to her face, transforming it with desire from plain to quite extraordinary. Adam kissed her, teasing open her lips with the tip of his tongue to taste the sweetness of her mouth. She tasted of parma violets.

Her large breasts flattened against his chest as she pressed herself to him, the generous discs around her nipples puckering into an insistent hardness. Lifting one breast in his hand, Adam moved his lips to its centre, drawing the tumescent teat into his mouth with a low moan of delight.

Rhiordan shuddered as his fingers dug into her flesh, kneading the orb of her breast into a cone. Tangling her fingers into his hair, she sought in vain to control his movements, gasping as his teeth grazed the sensitive tip. His lips drew on her nipple, creating an answering tug deep in her womb, and she had to gather all her willpower to ease him away.

His eyes were dark and unfocused as he looked at her.

'What?'

Rhiordan placed her fingers gently against his lips, quietening him. 'I want you on your knees,' she told him.

Though her voice quavered, betraying her own arousal, there was sufficient command in her tone to make Adam take notice. Suppressing his instinct to ignore her demand, to crush her to him and bend her sweetly to his own will, he found himself dropping to his knees at her feet.

Looking up at her, he could sense her excitement. She quivered, barely perceptibly, but enough to create an answering surge of lust deep in his belly. On an eye-level with the apex of her thighs, Adam gazed at the neat triangle of wiry black hair and imagined parting her legs, opening her with his thumbs to reveal the warm, wet well of her womanhood.

Sensing that it was part of Rhiordan's pleasure to set the pace, he forced himself to wait, confident that all would be revealed when the time was right. He could wait . . . just.

Rhiordan took her time, half closing her eyes so that she could feel the pleasurable anticipation trickle slowly through her body, from her head to her toes. The sun felt warm against her nakedness, yet the light breeze tickled her skin, making her feel exposed, yet deliciously lascivious.

All she had to do was give Adam a sign, and he would touch and kiss her – that would be all it would take to send her spinning into the vortex of sensation which would ultimately lead to climax. It was tempting, but she didn't want it to end just yet. She wanted to wring every last ounce of excitement from this encounter, and she wanted to leave Adam eager for more.

Slowly, she ran her palms lovingly across her belly and up to her breasts. Adam swallowed as she lifted her breasts in her hands and caressed herself, stroking the elongated peaks of her nipples gently with her thumbs.

'Touch yourself,' she whispered.

Adam wasn't sure he had heard right.

'What?' he breathed, his eyes still fixed on the rhythmic movement of her fingers against her breasts.

'Hold your cock in one hand and stroke it with the other. You know how.'

His eyes rose to lock with hers. Surely she didn't expect him to be content with masturbation after all this?

'Go on,' she coaxed him, 'I want to watch you.'

It was not so much her words as the curious light in her eyes that made him comply. She watched avidly as he enclosed the swollen shaft of his penis in his fist. It felt hot and inflexible, undeniably potent.

'Stroke it,' Rhiordan whispered.

As if to encourage him, she allowed one of her own hands to flutter down, over her belly towards her pussy. Adam watched as her middle finger burrowed into the hidden purse. He could smell the faint, spicy scent of feminine arousal and as she withdrew her finger, he saw that it was shiny with the dew of her body.

His throat tightened and his breathing became shallow as he watched her raise her finger to her lips and suck the tip between them. Slowly, holding his eye, she drew the length of her finger into her mouth, sucking it clean.

Adam imagined it was the slender shaft of his cock sliding into the plump, cushiony gateway to Rhiordan's mouth and almost came there and then. Her eyes flickered to his crotch and Adam immediately began to circle the circumcised tip of his penis with the thumb and forefinger of one hand.

The sensitive skin felt like velvet beneath his fingerpad, so fine he could barely feel it. Imagining it sinking into the dark, welcoming depths of Rhiordan's sex, he ran his fist slowly along the shaft, his palm a poor substitute for the cleated walls of her most intimate passage.

'Oh yes,' Rhiordan whispered, her eyes fixed on the clear teardrop of fluid that seeped from the crease. 'That's beautiful. Lie back.'

Adam obeyed her with alacrity, eager to have his own hand replaced by the cool softness of hers, but Rhiordan had other ideas. Once he was prone, she stood over him, facing down his body and placing her feet firmly either side of his shoulders.

Adam found himself looking up into her vulva. Her inner lips were swollen and almost scarlet, suffused with the rosy glow of desire. They shimmered moistly, filling his vision, the deep, dark indentation that led to the channel of her vagina opening and closing rhythmically, as if blowing him kisses. Beckoning him inside her.

Adam's cock jerked eagerly as she dropped lightly to her knees so that she was squatting over his face. He felt surrounded by the sight and scent of her, overwhelmed by a sensory overload. As she lowered herself on to his face, he opened his mouth in anticipation of the first taste of her.

Rhiordan moaned as his tongue lapped against the slippery folds of her labia, searching for her clitoris. As he flicked his tongue against it, she squirmed against his face before leaning forward, taking her weight on her hands so that he could breathe.

Adam's cock bobbed against her cheek, as if with a life of its own it sought the moist warmth of her mouth. He sighed against her pliant sex-flesh as her lips enclosed the bulb of his penis and her tongue traced the slit, lapping at the fluid that leaked from the end.

His testicles swelled and grew hot as the spunk built up. Rhiordan cupped them in her cool, soft palm and squeezed, so gently, making him squirm and thrust his tongue deeper into the dark channel of her sex.

All his senses seemed to be heightened: he could smell the soft, loamy soil beneath the grass cushioning his prone body, vying with the scent and taste of Rhiordan's aroused body. The sun beat down on his exposed legs and arms and he could hear the busy drone of insects in the long grass surrounding them. Above them, the birds continued their song, oblivious to the human passion that was now building to a crescendo on the ground below them.

Vaguely, he was aware of the breeze against his skin and the incongruous chirrup of a grasshopper close to his head. Then he felt the hard little button of Rhiordan's clitoris buck against his tongue as she vaulted over the precipice and all his concentration was taken up with pleasuring her, prolonging her orgasm for as long as he possibly could.

Just when he thought her climax would never end, she sank down onto his cock and began to suck for all she was worth, tipping him over the edge so that all his sensation was focused on that slender rod of flesh which seemed to be about to erupt.

Climbing off, Rhiordan crawled next to Adam so that she could milk him with her hands, lips and tongue. With a huge effort, Adam hauled himself up so that he was propped on his elbows, able to see what was going on. The sight of Rhiordan's plump, flushed body crouched over his cock, all her attention focused on the ultimate fulfilment of his pleasure, made the sensations more intense, the benefit of the visual stimulus contributing to the overload of feeling.

He was going to climax. He could feel the cum boiling in his testicles, preparing to surge along the iron-hard shaft that was pumping furiously in and out of Rhiordan's mouth. Feeling how close he was, she suddenly sat back on her heels, startling him as the cool air touched his hot, saliva-soaked cock.

She smiled beatifically at him as she squatted on the grass beside him, her body unashamedly open, displayed for his pleasure. Adam's breath began to hurt in his chest as he sought to maintain the momentum of his gathering climax, afraid that she was about to leave him unsatisfied.

'Do it all over my tits,' she said, her voice gravelly

with lust. 'Spurt all over me . . .'

Her words were enough. With a shuddering gasp, Adam took his cock in his hands and masturbated frantically. The first gush of ejaculate spattered her breasts. Rhiordan lay back on the grass, sighing, rubbing the hot, viscous fluid into her skin with her hands. Adam reared up on to his knees and directed his ejaculation over her neck and lips, gasping as the last droplets emerged.

Rhiordan licked greedily around her lips while her hands sought the pulsating bud of her clitoris. Adam lay back exhausted, and watched as she masturbated herself to another climax, envious of her swift recovery.

As she came for a second time, he leaned over her and kissed her on the mouth. The taste of her mixed with the salty tang of his own freshly spilt semen clung to his lips as their tongues collided. Hungrily, they clung together, determined to eke out every last drop of pleasure before, at last, they both lay back, sated.

Side by side beneath the benevolent sun, they breathed heavily as they waited for their hearts to slow and their temperatures to cool.

'Adam?' Rhiordan murmured sleepily after a few minutes.

'Hmm?'

'Do you think Susie is beautiful?' She rolled on to her side and lifted herself up on one elbow so that she could see his face as he replied.

Adam stiffened. He didn't like the turn this conversation was taking. It woke him rudely from a comfortable post-orgasmic stupor.

'She's very pretty,' he replied cautiously.

He sensed Rhiordan's withdrawal and wondered what it was she had expected him to say.

'Do you fancy her?'

Adam opened his eyes and stared at her.

'Honestly?'

'Of course!'

He grinned. 'Not really. I like my women volup-tuous.'

'Oh?'

'Mmm.'

He rolled over and eased her down on to her back on the grass, silencing her with a kiss. Settling himself comfortably with his head on her breasts, he closed his eyes again, contented.

Chapter Four

ON FRIDAY, DIANA laid the table for dinner herself, using the time to prepare herself mentally for Sebastian Semple's arrival. When she had finished, she stood back and gave the dining room a critical look.

The lamps she had placed around the room gave off a muted, intimate glow which softened the functional style of the dining room, turning it into something quite cosy. The pine table had been covered with a crisp damask cloth in a rich, clotted cream colour and laid with newly polished silver cutlery and the best china. In the centre, Diana had arranged a mixed bouquet of fresh flowers, cutting the stems so that they would not obstruct the guests' view of the others around the table.

She sighed, aware of a heaviness in her heart. Whatever happened tonight, she knew it was inevitable that Susie would leave the farm as planned next week. She could only hope that meeting the man who had promised her daughter so much would set her own mind at rest about the project.

She had asked Mrs Evans to make a special meal in honour of Sebastian's visit. She and Jack had discussed the situation and decided that they would go out of their way to welcome the photographer, in the hope that he might relax and let them get to know him.

Adam had been dismissive of the whole thing. 'Are you sure you need me around? I had planned to take Rhiordan out into Haverfordwest on Friday. There's a band on she wants to see.'

'Rhiordan? You're a fast worker, son,' Jack said, the reluctant note of admiration in his voice earning him an irritated glance from his new wife.

'It's nothing serious, Dad, just a bit of fun.'

Diana shook her head. 'Watch your step, Adam. If I know Megan Davis she'll be monitoring this new relationship of her daughter's like a field commander.'

'She'll have you hog-tied before you know it,' Jack added with a laugh.

Adam looked uncomfortable. 'That's crazy! Rhiordan doesn't see it like that.'

'Are you sure?' Diana asked him.

'Sure I'm sure,' he said, frowning.

'Well, bring the girl to dinner on Friday – it might help to break the ice with this photographer,' Jack suggested. 'We'd like you to be here, Adam. You're one of the family, after all.'

Outnumbered and outmanoeuvred, Adam gave in.

Now Diana could see Susie riding back towards the house on Ginger, in plenty of time to shower and change in anticipation of Sebastian's arrival. Glancing at her watch, she decided she would nip into the shower herself, before Susie took all the hot water. There was nothing else she could do here.

He came – an hour late – armed with flowers for Diana and Susie and a bottle of vintage port for Jack.

'I'm sorry I'm late – I swear my taxi driver was a distant relation of Herman from *The Munsters*! I guess it must be all the in-breeding that goes on in them there hills!'

Diana smiled tightly and watched as he kissed Susie enthusiastically on both cheeks and held her away from him, eyeing her up and down critically.

'Just as lovely as I remember!'

Susie was wearing a black jersey dress with shoe-string straps. The fabric clung to her body, moving sinuously with her, making it clear she wasn't wearing any underwear. Jack had been horrified, but by the time the crafty girl had emerged from her room, their guest was already halfway up the drive and it had been too late to send her back to change. Now she glowed in the face of his praise.

'Thank you,' she said, accepting the compliment as her due. 'Sebastian, this is my mother, Diana Jones . . . sorry, Diana Corcoran, and her husband, Jack.'

To her surprise, Diana found herself subjected to the same treatment as Susie. As Sebastian's assessing gaze slid over her body, she didn't know whether to feel flattered, or to slap his handsome face. A quick glance at Jack's smouldering expression and she realised he thought she should have gone with the latter instinct.

'It's not difficult to see where Susie gets her fabulous looks from,' Sebastian said, predictably.

'And her common sense,' Jack put in, stepping forward so that Sebastian was forced to let go of Diana and shake his hand.

From the way he was unable to hide a wince, Diana guessed that Jack had made clear what he thought of Sebastian's appraisal of his wife. She glanced at Adam and had to look away quickly to stop herself from smiling.

'And this is my son,' Jack said.

'Adam Corcoran.' Adam didn't bother to move from the doorjamb he was leaning against, and Sebastian's eyes passed quickly over him, clearly judging him to be of no importance.

'And who is *this*?' he said, treating Rhiordan to the full wattage of his smile.

Dazzled, Rhiordan giggled. 'Rhiordan Davis,' she said. 'I'm Susie's friend – and Adam's, of course,' she added hastily, feeling his eyes on her back as she stepped forward.

If she was hoping for a hug, she was to be disappointed, for at that moment Mrs Evans appeared at the doorway, dressed in her mac and headscarf.

'I'll be off now, Mrs Corcoran,' she said, buttoning her coat. 'I've left the dinner on the stove – it's not *too* dried up,' she added, casting Sebastian a malevolent glance. 'My Gwyn is here to pick me up now, see, so you'll have to serve yourselves.'

'That's quite all right, Mrs Evans. I'm sure the girls will help me. Thank you for staying for as long as you have.'

Sebastian made a face as Susie ushered him into the drawing room. 'It looks like I've upset the hired help,' he said, dropping his voice so that no one else could hear.

'Don't worry,' she whispered back. 'I'll see you in a minute.'

Summoned with a glance by Diana, Susie left Sebastian alone with Jack and Adam.

'What?' she said defiantly as Diana raised her eyebrows at her when she walked into the kitchen.

'He is very late, Susie,' Diana remarked.

'I'm sure that's not his fault. After all, he's had to

66

travel a long way. You shouldn't let Mrs Evans be so rude to our guests, Mummy.'

Diana bit her tongue, determined not to make things worse by being drawn into an argument. She looked at the meal already set out on plates on the top of the stove and sighed. Emergency measures were clearly called for.

'Make some fresh gravy, Susie. Perhaps you'd carry through the starter, Rhiordan dear, while I call everyone into the dining room.'

As soon as the girls had the tasks she had set them underway, Diana went to join the men in the drawing room. Jack had opened a bottle of dry sherry and she took the glass he offered her gratefully. Sebastian was standing by the window looking amused, if mildly uncomfortable, while Adam glowered from the fireplace. Diana felt her heart sink as she realised that without her restraining influence, Adam and Jack had apparently lost no time in making assumptions about their guest, and a disagreement had already occurred.

'Well,' she said brightly, 'dinner is almost ready. Shall we go through?'

She had seated Susie and Rhiordan on either side of Jack at one end of the table, while Adam and Sebastian flanked her at the other. As they ate the Welsh bread and soup that Mrs Evans had prepared, Sebastian seemed to recover his equilibrium and quickly reverted to what Diana supposed was his usual charming form.

'Susie is very excited at the prospect of moving to London, Mr Semple,' she began as her daughter cleared away the dishes.

'Call me Sebastian, please. She should be excited, Diana. Susie has a wonderful future ahead of her.'

He smiled at Susie as she returned, carrying the main course with her.

Diana waited until she had gone back to the kitchen for more plates before continuing. 'What exactly do you have in mind for her?'

No doubt conscious of the men's eyes on him, Sebastian appeared to consider his response carefully. 'A very structured introduction to the industry. It's very important that we work to create the right image for Susie before we jump in with a portfolio. She'll be taught how to walk, talk, hold herself, as well as attending make-up classes, hair and grooming – everything you might expect a top model to know. A complete makeover, in fact.'

'You mean you're going to take the Susie out of Susie?' Adam drawled, earning himself a furious glare from the subject of the conversation. 'Gee, thanks, sis,' he said as she banged his plate down in front of him, spilling fat, green peas on to the pristine damask cloth and making her mother wince.

'Not exactly,' Sebastian said, directing his comments to Diana and ignoring the other man. 'You see, what people don't realise is that models are created, not born. Susie has the raw potential to make it to the very top of the profession. It's my job to turn potential into—'

'Bankability?'

Sebastian shot Adam a scornful glance.

'That is one aspect of the game, yes.'

'Of course it is,' Susie put in quickly. 'Sebastian isn't going to help me for nothing, is he?'

'I don't suppose he is,' Adam said softly, holding her eye until she blushed.

Diana groaned inwardly. This wasn't what she had planned at all. The man was hardly going to let down

68

his guard and let her get to know him while Adam was being so hostile. And as for Jack – he'd barely said two words all evening, and yet his look spoke volumes, none of it favourable.

'I suppose what Mr Semple ... sorry, *Sebastian*, is trying to say, albeit politely, is that Susie is his product, and he has to find the best way to market her.'

The wide smile Sebastian turned on her held not a little gratitude. '*Exactly*, Diana – how succinctly put.'

He seemed to feel that he had been let off the hook somehow and he relaxed visibly. Diana smiled politely at him and offered the gravy boat. It seemed that there was little else she could do.

Susie watched from beneath her lashes as they ate dinner. She could not believe how rude everyone was being to their guest. Not so much Diana – she was ever the gracious hostess. Hopefully only Susie could sense the icy reserve that her mother was struggling to keep in check as she chatted politely with Sebastian.

Rhiordan was keeping very quiet, but then she was clearly preoccupied with Adam at the moment. Adam. How dare he presume to make any comment on her plans? What had any of it got to do with him?

Susie fumed silently. She hadn't wanted Adam and Rhiordan here this evening in the first place; as far as she was concerned, it really was stretching family togetherness too far. Besides, it was embarrassing to have to watch her so-called best friend and her step-brother canoodling with each other across the table.

As she watched, they caught each other's eyes and smiled, excluding the rest of the table. A hint of some unnameable emotion travelled coolly along the length of Susie's spine. Surely they weren't sleeping together already?

Susie regarded them closely. She could see now that Rhiordan's left hand was under the table. Knocking her napkin off the table, Susie leaned down to retrieve it so that she could look underneath. Sure enough, Rhiordan's hand was resting possessively on Adam's leg, which was pressed tightly against hers. As she watched, Rhiordan's fingers moved against his thigh, tracing light circles against the fabric of his trousers. Susie felt her stomach muscles contract, as if an elevator had just plummeted from her solar plexus to her pubis, inexplicably making her mouth and throat dry.

As she straightened, she inadvertently caught Adam's eye. She flushed as she realised he knew exactly what she had been doing, and he was amused by her discomfiture. The pig! She glared at him, then snapped her eyes away, turning her attention resolutely to Sebastian.

It didn't make sense to her that she should feel so incredibly uncomfortable at the thought of Adam being with Rhiordan, but there was no denying that her skin burned and her stomach roiled uncomfortably at the thought.

'Have you found me somewhere to stay yet, Sebastian?' she asked, forcing her attention on to the far more attractive prospect of her own immediate future.

'There are just a few more details to sort out. I'll let you know as soon as I can so you'll be able to give your lovely mother a contact address, which I'm sure will make her feel better about your departure.' He flashed Diana a winning smile before turning his attention back to Susie.

For the rest of the evening Sebastian flirted discreetly

with his protégé, Rhiordan and Adam appeared to be lost in a world of their own, and Diana and Jack sent each other pained looks along the length of the table. Everyone was relieved when the meal was at an end and they could move from the dining room.

Jack announced that he would help Diana make coffee. Adam and Rhiordan excused themselves abruptly, and Susie was left looking wistfully after them. She overheard Rhiordan's whispered exhortation for him to 'hurry up'.

'I've got a surprise for you,' she said, giggling.

'Yeah?' Adam's attention was focused fully on her, so he did not notice Susie watching them. 'Can't wait,' he said, taking Rhiordan by the hand and pulling her through the front door.

In the drawing room, Susie moved to the window to watch as they walked arm in arm towards the car Jack had recently provided for his son. She couldn't understand the pang of envy she felt as she watched Adam put his arm around Rhiordan's shoulders. She had no feelings for Adam, aside from irritation and the occasional fury. The way it made her feel to watch him with Rhiordan made no sense; there was no reason why it should pain her to see them together.

Perhaps the feeling was more to do with Rhiordan than Adam. After all, the girl was supposed to be her best friend, and they had barely exchanged two words all evening. But as they disappeared from view, Adam's arm still round Rhiordan, Susie found she could not suppress a sigh. It was such an easy, protective gesture . . .

'I wish I had my camera with me right now,' Sebastian murmured in her ear. He put his hand on her bare shoulder in a pale imitation of the embrace she had been watching through the window. She felt a pang of something suspiciously like loss, then she pulled herself together. It was only a childish hurt at being excluded from Rhiordan's surprise, nothing to do with Adam at all. Turning her face up to look at Sebastian, she smiled brightly, forcing the expression into her eyes.

The look in the older man's eyes made Susie's heart skip a beat. It fuelled the strange, unfamiliar yearning that watching Adam and Rhiordan had triggered and sent a warm, treacly sensation through her body.

Suddenly, she was conscious that they were alone in the room. Sebastian was standing very close, so close that she could sense his body, not touching her, but mere centimetres away, as if his hardness imprinted itself on her softness without the need for the slightest physical contact. There was a tension in him she had never noticed before, a coiled emotion barely under control, which frightened her a little, even while it excited her.

His eyes, normally a cool blue, had darkened to a luminous sapphire, his pupils dilated and fixed. She could feel his breath against her cheek and could smell the scent of hair gel and *cK one* cologne. The combination made her feel ever so slightly queasy.

'If I could capture the look you had on your face just now . . .'

He touched his fingertips against the length of her hair, following the shape of her face with his eyes as if calculating the angle of light he would need to photograph her. Almost imperceptibly, he leaned forward so that his face swam slightly out of focus. His mouth was so close to hers, the brush of his breath made her lower lip quiver involuntarily. She thought that he would kiss her, and knew that it was what she wanted.

72

Just then, the sound of footsteps penetrated her consciousness, and she moved away from him, embarrassed as much by her own feelings as by her mother's imminent arrival. Glancing through the window, she saw the tail lights of Adam's car disappearing round the bend of the drive and envied him his easy, uninhibited intimacy with Rhiordan. She had never felt like that with a man before and she rued her inexperience. Something told her that Sebastian was used to that in a woman.

'Coffee?' Diana said as Jack laid the tray on the low table between the sofas.

The look she gave her daughter was shrewd and Susie felt her cheeks suffuse with colour. Diana had always had an uncanny knack of divining her innermost thoughts – even the ones she wanted to keep secret. It was a finely honed mother's instinct that Susie had often cursed, never more so than now.

To cover her embarrassment, she went to pour the coffee for everyone, conscious of Sebastian's eyes on her too, though for a very different reason to Diana's.

'It was very good of you to invite me to stay here in your home,' Sebastian said politely, lightening the atmosphere as they all sat down.

'Not at all – you've come a long way,' Diana said graciously.

'Do you come from London?' Jack asked, making Susie wonder whether Diana had told him to make more of an effort while they were in the kitchen together making coffee.

'Born and bred,' Sebastian replied, making himself comfortable beside Susie on one sofa.

As the small talk continued, Susie found herself supremely conscious of his arm along the length of the sofa, not touching her, but oh, so close. She watched his mouth as he talked, his well-shaped lips forming words she barely heard. All her senses were focused on Sebastian – the way he looked, the smell of him, his sheer physical presence – so that everything and everyone else appeared to her as though through a film of water. She had never felt anything remotely like this before, and it puzzled her.

As Sebastian, Jack and Diana continued a desultory conversation, Susie studied the man sitting next to her from the corner of her eye, trying to analyse the feeling. Of course, he was terrifically handsome. His dirty-blond hair was thick and fashionably overlong, caught back in a thin leather thong at the nape of his neck. Thus his face was exposed, emphasising the jagged thrust of his cheekbones and the aquiline length of his nose above a full, mobile mouth. His eyes were narrow, but generously fringed with dark blond lashes below thick, well-groomed eyebrows and his skin was smooth and tanned a honey-gold colour which reminded Susie of crème brûlée.

Though he was wiry rather than muscular, he was taller than her, and broad enough to make her feel small and feminine. His hands, resting on the fine material of his trousered thigh, were fine-boned and sensitive looking, his long fingers tapering into neat, oval nails, his knuckles dusted with a sprinkling of fine blond hairs. Susie imagined those fingers brushing across the surface of her naked skin and shivered involuntarily.

'Cold?' Sebastian murmured.

Susie blinked, suddenly realising that all eyes in the room were on her, and wondering how long she had been the focus of their attention. Were her thoughts plain for everyone to see?

'Er ... no, not at all,' she stammered, aware of Sebastian's cool, amused eyes scanning her face. Did he know how his nearness was affecting her? It was obvious that he did, and Susie felt she would die of embarrassment.

'Perhaps you'd like to show me round your lovely garden before it gets too cold outside?' he suggested.

'Better wrap up first,' Diana said, eyeing Susie's skimpy dress dubiously.

Realising that her mother would be only too happy for her to take their guest for a walk if it meant covering up her semi-nakedness, Susie left the room in search of a sweater.

It was a relief to get away from Sebastian for a few moments; his closeness was simply too overwhelming. Susie ran up the stairs to her room and pulled out a lacy cotton knit which covered her bare shoulders and arms. She felt less vulnerable now, more in control as she prepared to meet up with him in the hallway.

The feeling did not last long, for his eyes assessed her as she walked down the stairs, making her feel clumsy and gawky, liable to trip and take a fall. Relieved to reach the bottom of the stairs in one piece, she smiled brittlely and walked swiftly to the front door. Stepping out into the cool night air was a relief, and she breathed in deeply, catching the night-scent of her mother's flower garden on the soft breeze.

Sebastian followed her outside and on to the paved area beneath the drawing room windows. Conscious of Diana and Jack still sitting on the sofa, Susie walked quickly on, and down the steps that led to the lawn.

'You have a big place here,' he commented as he drew level with her.

'Yes. It's been in my mother's family for generations.'

'How quaint.'

She glanced at him, suspecting that he was laughing at her, but he merely smiled and put his arm around her shoulders. Susie stiffened, aware that this was what she had envied when she watched Rhiordan and Adam's departure. But Adam's arm across Rhiordan's shoulders had looked friendly as well as intimate. She hadn't had time to become friendly with Sebastian; in fact she hardly knew him at all, and as soon as she could, she moved out of his reach, giving herself some space. There were too many conflicting feelings competing for space in her mind, and whilst a part of her yearned for the physical closeness to him, another part of her held back, cowering.

'There really isn't much to see near the house,' she said, dismayed to hear that her voice had taken on a breathy, light quality; it was quite unlike her. 'I . . . I mean . . . in the morning we could take a walk, if you like, or ride . . .' she trailed off as Sebastian shuddered.

'Ride? Do you mean *horses*?'

'Well, yes . . .' He looked so horrified at the idea that she had to laugh. 'Believe me, if you lived here you'd have to ride or you'd go crazy.'

'Yet another reason why I'm thankful that I *don't* live here! And nor will you for much longer, Susie. Remember – you're heading for the bright lights, the fast track—Jesus, what's that?' he yelped, stepping back hurriedly.

He held up one foot to discover that his designer trainers were filmed with squelchy mud. Susie laughed.

'Don't worry, it's only mud. I suppose you could say that's another of London's attractions, isn't it? Paved streets?'

'Exactly, my dear. You are too exotic a bird to be

76

incarcerated in a land of crows. Shall we head back to the house?'

Susie nodded, still amused by his reaction to a bit of mud. This time when he put his arm around her shoulders, she did not move away. Encouraged, he manoeuvred her so that she was tucked up against him, so close she could feel his heart beating against the side of her breast. The fluttery feeling returned, making her feel breathless again.

'You are going to love the city. There's so much energy, so much vigour. Once you get there, you'll wonder how you stood all this for so long.' He made a sweeping gesture with his free arm which encompassed the whole of the farm.

Because it is my home, a still, small voice said mischievously inside Susie's head, but she pushed it away, refusing to listen. Sebastian was putting into words what she herself had always known. She wasn't cut out for life in rural Pembrokeshire. If she became a farmer's wife, she'd make that farmer very unhappy. It was only the thought of leaving Diana that made her doubt, just for a moment, the wisdom of what she was doing. That was all. It was perfectly natural.

'You're right – I can't wait!'

It was obviously the right thing to say, for Sebastian seemed to relax. He laughed. 'First we'll take the girl out of the country, then we'll take the country out of the girl,' he told her flippantly.

'I thought that couldn't be done?'

They had reached the back of the house, where French doors led into the rear hall. Sebastian turned her to face him, his expression serious.

'That's exactly what we *are* going to do, Susie. I'm going to mould you into the image of a star. When I've finished with you, even you won't recognise the face that stares back at you from the mirror in the mornings.'

For a moment, his intensity frightened her, and she laughed nervously. 'I'm not sure I'd like that,' she said uncertainly.

Sebastian cupped her chin in one hand and turned her face this way and that. His eyes raked her skin, her nose, her eyes, her hair, before settling on her mouth.

'I'll teach you to like it,' he murmured, his eyes never leaving the soft, tremulous pout of her lower lip. 'I can see that there's a great deal I can teach you . . .'

Susie held her breath, every muscle, every sinew rigid with a mixture of apprehension and undeniable excitement. His lips descended so slowly on to hers that she thought she would pass out with the wanting.

The first touch of his mouth against hers was electrifying, sending a jolt right through her. He still held her fast by the chin so that nothing touched but their lips, concentrating all sensation in one place.

Susie felt her eyelids flutter and involuntarily close. As if of their own accord, her lips parted on a sigh of surrender, her mouth opening beneath the pressure of his, inviting him to deepen the kiss. He didn't, and she felt the frustration would make her legs buckle beneath her.

Her breasts tingled, her hardening nipples straining towards the hard wall of his chest, so tantalisingly close, and she felt the tender folds of her sex growing moist. A deep, strong pulse began to beat between her thighs and she swayed towards him, overcome by a sudden, unfamiliar weakness.

She thought he would crush her to him and kiss her deeply, properly; she expected to feel his arms slide around her shoulders, pulling her close. Instead, he pushed her gently away, smiling enigmatically as her eyes snapped open and her unfulfilled lips formed a small circle of thwarted expectation.

'We should go in,' he said. 'Your mother will be looking out for you.'

Susie allowed herself to be comforted by the note of regret that coloured his tone, and was grateful to him for not losing his head as she could so easily have done.

'Yes, yes of course,' she agreed, aware that her voice, now smoky and soft, had dropped an octave.

'We'll have more space, more time when you move into town,' he told her softly as she opened the door and stepped inside.

'Yes,' she whispered, 'yes, we will.'

As they reached the underside of the stairs, he suddenly reached one arm around her and pulled her backwards against his body. Susie gasped, aware of the potent line of his obviously erect penis pressing urgently against the crease of her bottom.

'I've come to take you away from all this,' he said, his breath hot against her ear as his hands explored her breasts, kneading and squeezing and flattening her burgeoning nipples against her chest. 'Oh, Susie – you're going to have such a good time. You have no idea.'

His tongue lapped wetly at her ear, making her shiver convulsively. His none too gentle caresses were making her feel weak and breathless and so very wet. Yet her mouth and throat were so dry she could not utter a sound.

She drew in her breath as one hand smoothed down her belly to trace the small hummock of her mons beneath the tight jersey dress. Then he kissed her cheek and moved away from her, leaving her shaking.

'We'd better rejoin your parents,' he said, his voice cool and controlled, as if nothing had happened between them.

She stared at him, and he raised a quizzical eyebrow at her. The strength of her arousal seemed to vibrate in her veins and she wondered how on earth she could face Diana and Jack without them knowing at once what they had been doing.

Sebastian's face was cast in shadow so she could not read his expression. Guessing that he was nowhere near as affected by what he had just done to her as she was, Susie struggled to pull herself together. She didn't want him to think she was a silly, virginal little girl, afraid of her own sexuality. He didn't need to know that she had never allowed anyone to touch her so intimately, nor had she dreamed that such rough treatment would turn her on so much.

Now was not the time to think about it, though; there were more pressing matters to attend to. Like getting through the rest of the evening with some semblance of normality.

Mustering a smile, she straightened her shoulders and smoothed down her dress.

'More coffee, I think, don't you?' she said, proud of the way her voice affected to be cool and light.

She thought she detected a hint of admiration in his eyes as she passed him, and instinctively stored the information away for future reference. It might be useful later on to know how to handle Sebastian Semple – especially if she was going to allow him to literally handle her.

The thought made her smile, even as it recalled the feel of his hands on her breasts and belly and the wet, lascivious movement of his tongue in her ear. And she

80

wondered, for the first time in her young life, if she might have taken on more than she was ready to cope with.

It was a sobering thought, and a slightly frightening one. But as she walked into the drawing room, Susie was aware that her overriding feeling was not apprehension, nor fear. It was sheer mouth-drying, knee-trembling excitement – and that was the scariest part of all.

Chapter Five

ADAM GLANCED ACROSS at Rhiordan and smiled. The girl virtually buzzed with the pleasure of having a secret. It was almost childlike, but there was nothing remotely childlike about the woman sitting beside him.

His eyes roamed her full bosom appreciatively. The silky green blouse she had chosen to wear for the evening wasn't particularly eye-catching, but having had first-hand experience of what was beneath the demure, high-buttoned frontage, Adam had been admiring it all evening.

Thank God she had been there at dinner – at least she had distracted him from the distasteful sight of that photographer creep leering at Susie. It had put him off his dinner, watching another guy go through his moves so blatantly. Worse, Susie seemed to be swallowing every line, lapping up the attention, preening herself and fluttering her eyelashes at the guy. Adam wondered what she thought she was doing, or if she even realised the signals she was sending out. Surely she couldn't be that naïve? It had been enough to make him want to puke.

'What's this secret, then, Rhiordan?' he asked hastily, not wanting even to think about what was going on back at the farm now that they had left.

'Wait and see,' she replied enigmatically.

He sighed. 'How about a clue?'

'No way. Haven't you heard of patience in Canada?'

He snorted. 'No one's been subjected to your little games over there! Hey!' he protested as she punched him playfully on the upper arm. 'That almost hurt!'

'You'll regret it if you carry on,' she told him ominously. 'You know what curiosity did to the cat.'

'Okay, okay.' They drove in silence for a few minutes. 'I am going to like this surprise though, aren't I?'

Instead of answering him, Rhiordan leaned across and ran her tongue around the outer edge of his ear, making his hands falter on the steering wheel.

'Cut that out,' he snapped at her as he corrected the car.

Without warning, his mood changed, and suddenly he felt thoroughly pissed off. 'You'd better tell me what's going on or I might just drop you home and call it a night.' He caught Rhiordan's surprised glance and instantly felt ashamed.

'Moody bastard, aren't you?' she said.

Adam scowled. *Not normally*, he wanted to say, *only since I met my infuriating new 'sister'*. His scowl deepened. How come Susie had got under his skin? She was nothing more than an over-indulged child who probably deserved the fall he guessed was coming to her. There was no logical reason, after the way she had treated him, why he should give a damn. He didn't, for Chrissakes! Susie Jones meant nothing to him. If it wasn't for the fact that he was inextricably linked to her now through his father's marriage to her mother, he'd never even have given her so much as a second glance.

Certainly, there was no reason to take out his

irritation with Susie on Rhiordan, whose company to date had offered him nothing but sweetness and light.

'I'm sorry,' he said, covering her hand with his and giving it a reassuring squeeze. 'Guess I'm a bit tired is all.'

She smiled at him and he knew he was forgiven. She was such an uncomplicated girl, and Adam felt ashamed of himself for his earlier bad temper.

'It's okay. Actually, you're probably right – I ought to give you some inkling of what I've got planned. Just so that you're prepared, you know?'

'That sounds ominous!'

She shrugged. 'Not really. It's no big deal – I wanted you to meet my mum, that's all.'

For a few seconds the silence hung heavily between them. Adam recalled what Jack and Diana had said about Megan Davis, warning him off. He knew that if he wanted to continue to see her daughter, he would have to meet her formally at some point, but he had wanted to plan their first meeting carefully, not have it sprung on him like this.

'You don't mind do you?' Rhiordan said, breaking the uncomfortable silence that had fallen between them.

'No . . . you know I'd be happy to meet your mother, Rhiordan, but . . . it's real late and—'

'She said she'd wait up, to bring you in whatever time we got back from the Corcorans'.'

Adam glanced at her. 'It's all arranged, then?'

'Well . . . yes.' Her shrug was slightly sheepish and Adam realised that she had deliberately not given him advance warning, probably anticipating his response.

'Why didn't you say something earlier? You've known all along that this was how the evening was going to end. You could have warned me.'

84

'Warned you?' Rhiordan looked genuinely perplexed. 'Whatever for?'

Adam tried to find the right words and failed. Maybe Rhiordan didn't know about her mother's reputation for trying to marry her daughter off. Worse, maybe Rhiordan was hoping for the same thing?

Adam went hot and cold at the thought. All this time he had been anticipating a quick, uncomplicated roll in the hay to round off the evening, while Rhiordan had been steering him towards some kind of commitment. Now she was bringing in the big guns in the form of her mother, springing it on him when he was least prepared. It was enough to make a guy paranoid.

She'll have you up the aisle with her daughter in no time. That's what Jack had said about Megan Davis. *Oh, hell!*

'I don't think tonight is such a good idea,' he said now. 'I'll drop you home and—'

'Adam,' Rhiordan cut him off sharply. 'What's the matter with you? From the way you're acting anyone would think you were frightened of meeting my mother.'

'Of course I'm not frightened of meeting her, I—'

'Well, then. She's expecting us, Adam. She'll be waiting up. I can hardly tell her that you got cold feet and decided not to come in, can I?'

Put like that, Adam saw he had no choice, not if he wanted to continue his relationship with Rhiordan. Her generous breasts pressed pliantly against his arm as she turned to kiss him on the cheek, and he knew that he didn't want it to end, not yet.

'All right,' he said grudgingly, just as they reached the edge of the village. 'But let's keep it short, Rhiordan. I was kind of looking forward to having you to myself for a while, y'know?'

'I know, love – you're not the only one with itchy pants.'

Adam burst out laughing at her casually crude turn of phrase and, to their mutual relief, the unaccustomed awkwardness between them passed.

Rhiordan lived on the opposite side of the village to the Jones Farm. Once a tied cottage to the now derelict manor house, the house was hidden from the road by a thick hedge. Turning into the gravelled driveway, Adam wondered for the first time about Rhiordan's family. They hadn't had much time for exchanging genealogies during their short time together.

'Is it just you and your mother living here?' he asked as they rounded the bend and the cottage came into view.

'Yes.' Unusually for Rhiordan, her answer was short and she did not expand on it.

'No father?' Adam probed, only half interested.

Rhiordan gave him a strange look.

'I suppose you've been listening to the village gossips,' she said wearily, going on before he could refute the allegation. 'There was one once, apparently. My mother isn't a conventional sort of person. You'll see.'

Adam switched off the engine. From what Jack and Diana had said, 'conventional' seemed exactly the sort of word he had expected to come to mind when he met Megan Davis. Perplexed, he jumped out of the car and followed Rhiordan into the house.

As they approached, he saw that the downstairs was in darkness. Aware of a small flicker of relief, he stopped Rhiordan at the door.

'It looks as though she's turned in – come on, we don't want to disturb her.'

'Oh, she's up,' Rhiordan answered, glancing up to where a soft light glowed welcomingly in an upstairs window.

Following her gaze, Adam frowned. 'But—'

His words were strangled by the sudden force of Rhiordan's mouth against his. Standing on tiptoe, she pressed herself against the length of his body and kissed him deeply.

Adam felt himself stir and harden. He could sense the warmth of her skin beneath the flimsy covering of her clothes and the melting of her soft flesh against the hard contours of his body. Rational thought fled as he allowed himself to sink into the delicious fog of arousal that enveloped them as she kissed him, her hands working between their bodies to stroke the hardness straining at his fly.

'Mmm,' he murmured as she drew back. 'More.'

'Come inside,' she whispered, 'it's getting cool out here.'

The door led directly into the kitchen. Inside, the cottage was warm and welcoming. Attempting to divert himself from the urgency of his desire, Adam forced himself to look around the room. Though it was reasonably large, the ceiling was low, built in a time when men were shorter, or considerably less claustrophobic than he felt as he closed the door behind him. He followed Rhiordan over to the large pine table in the centre of the room, stooping to avoid banging his head on the beams that ran across the ceiling. Seeing his discomfort, Rhiordan laughed.

'Mum's small like me, so we don't notice the low ceiling,' she said, pulling out a chair for him.

'I thought you said she'd be up,' Adam said, eyeing the chair dubiously.

'Sit down and stop your fussing!' Rhiordan pushed him gently towards the chair and swiftly planted herself in his lap as he obeyed.

For a few seconds, Adam hung on to his sense of foreboding at the thought of Rhiordan's mother appearing in the doorway like an avenging angel, but it didn't last long. The feel of Rhiordan's soft, plump buttocks moulding around the tumescent shaft of his trouser-clad penis was distraction enough, but when he turned his head and found himself on an eye-level with the cushiony globes of her satin-covered breasts, he knew he was lost.

'Mmm, I've been wanting to do this all evening!' he said, unbuttoning her blouse and sinking his face into her warm, moist cleavage.

She smelled of perfume and fresh sweat. Tracing little circles on her skin with the tip of his tongue, Adam delighted in the way goosebumps immediately rose up on her flesh, making her shiver. Lust vibrated right through her, and she squirmed exquisitely in his lap.

'Oh, you!' she said, tangling her fingers in the hair at the back of his head and pressing him closer to her.

Adam moved his head from side to side, kissing each breast in turn. Revelling in his position, he burrowed his tongue beneath the flimsy lace of her bra, seeking out the hard button of her nipple with his lips. As soon as he found it, he drew it slowly into his mouth, savouring every second.

Rhiordan moaned softly as the smooth flesh of her aureola sprang into life, puckering and swelling against his tongue. Sucking rhythmically at the teat, he rolled her other nipple between his thumb and forefinger, tweaking the sensitive flesh until she gasped.

Unsure whether she was begging him to stop, or

urging him to continue, Adam ignored her, concentrating solely on his own pleasure for a few moments. When, finally, he reluctantly came up for air, her mouth was waiting for him; hot and hungry and demanding more.

Folding his arms around her, Adam felt as though she was melting into his arms. She was so soft, so very feminine and he was overcome with a need for her so strong he had to rein in the urge to fling her across the sturdy pine table, part her thighs and enter her there and then.

'Is there somewhere we can go?' he asked her as they broke apart.

Rhiordan's dark eyes glittered, reflecting his need with a feral desire of her own.

'Wait here,' she said, the huskiness in her voice turning his innards to water.

Adam sighed as she slid slowly off his lap, caressing him deliberately as she moved away from him.

'Don't be long,' he begged her, making her smile.

She left him with an ache in his loins the like of which he hadn't experienced since he was in high school. Now that he was a man, he was used to taking his pleasures as and when he found them, and he realised as he sat there waiting for Rhiordan to reappear that he took for granted the ease with which he conducted his sex life.

He had always seemed to attract sexually rapacious women like a magnet. The kind of women who took uninhibited pleasure in their sexuality appeared to recognise that quality in him. Women like Rhiordan had populated his life and his bed from the moment he discovered the pleasures to be had there. He'd never had to be patient before, and it did not come easily to him.

Looking round the room, he only half saw the old Welsh dresser in the corner with the neatly displayed collection of spongewear. There were dried flowers strung up in bunches on the pan rack above his head and an ancient looking Aga took pride of place in the middle of the opposite wall.

Where had she got to? He glanced at the grandmother clock in the corner of the room and saw that she had been gone for ten minutes. Was this some kind of a joke? Impatient, Adam got to his feet, wincing as the chair scraped noisily on the quarry tiled floor. If that hadn't woken Mrs Davis then she must sleep the sleep of the dead!

That thought gave him an idea. If she really was such a heavy sleeper, maybe she wouldn't hear if he crept up to Rhiordan's room to find out what she was up to.

Once the idea had occurred to him, it wouldn't leave him alone. He waited a further five long minutes before deciding to put it into action.

Beyond the kitchen, the house was in darkness. To put on a light would have been to invite detection, so he moved slowly towards the stairs, feeling his way carefully along the rough plastered wall.

Like the rest of the house, the stairs were old and they creaked as soon as he put his weight on the first step, making him wince. He was committed now, though – if Mrs Davis woke up he would be hardpressed to explain what he was doing creeping up her stairs in the middle of the night.

With a philosophical shrug, Adam decided he might as well be hung for a sheep as a lamb. Allowing the soft glow of the upstairs light to guide him, he walked quickly to the top of the stairs, an anticipatory smile playing around his lips.

There were four doors confronting him, all partially ajar. The one straight ahead he guessed was a bathroom, but there was no way of knowing which of the other three led to Rhiordan's room. There seemed to be a soft light burning in every bedroom, spilling out on to the hallway in misty yellow puddles.

Tentatively, Adam pushed open the door to the bathroom, half expecting to find her there waiting for him. The room was empty. On the landing, he stood for a moment and listened. The silence had an expectant quality which made the blood pulse more strongly through his veins. He had the sense that she was waiting for him, maybe even watching him.

'Rhiordan,' he called softly.

A sound like a muted giggle reached him, and he turned towards its source. Smiling to himself, he tiptoed over to the door and slowly eased it open.

The first thing he saw was Rhiordan, standing by the window where she was spot-lit by the soft glow of a bedside lamp. She had changed into a filmy, baby blue negligée which barely reached below her pubis and struggled to meet in a single fastening across her naked breasts. There were tiny panties to match and high-heeled mules which elongated her shapely legs, throwing her into a slightly top-heavy, seductive stance. She looked absolutely gorgeous – sex on legs.

A slow smile spread across Adam's face as he ran his eyes over her, drinking her in. A delicious tension held him rigid, making him aware of every pulse, every breath as he looked at her.

'God, you're incredible,' he breathed.

'She is, isn't she?'

Adam's smile froze as he realised she was not alone. His attention had been totally focused on Rhiordan; it

91

hadn't occurred to him to look around the room. Now his heart skipped a beat as he turned slowly towards the satin-covered, king-sized bed which dominated the room. His pulse accelerated as he saw a small, plump, dark-haired woman, dressed in a scarlet basque and black stockings – and nothing else.

Her hair was black, worn in a short bob which formed a soft cloud around her face. The mouth that curved upward into an amused little smile was wide and generous, the lips full and cushiony, painted scarlet to match her finger- and toenails.

Dark eyes challenged him, as if half expecting him to turn and run. Adam glanced from her to Rhiordan, whose own eyes sparkled with mischief, tinged with excitement. Adam recognised the strength of her arousal and felt every nerve and sinew in his body respond. A rich and tantalising arousal uncurled slowly from the pit of his belly, its tentacles reaching along his limbs until he felt suffused with heat. A fine film of perspiration broke out over his skin, and his heart began to beat a little faster, making his jaw throb.

'Aren't you going to introduce me to your friend, Rhiordan?' the woman said, amusement colouring every lilting word. 'I think he deserves an introduction, at least, don't you?'

Without taking her eyes from Adam's face, Rhiordan nodded. 'Of course. This is Adam. Adam, this is my mother, Megan. I told you she would wait up for us.'

Though his body had responded at once, Adam's brain was slower to catch up.

'Pleased to meet you,' he murmured, his eyes sliding from daughter to mother and back again, registering the likeness . . . and the differences.

'Likewise,' Megan answered. 'But if all that Rhiordan

has told me about you is even half true, I'm quite sure that the pleasure is going to be all mine. You like to fuck, I hear?'

Adam felt the grin spreading across his face as the initial surprise wore off. Rhiordan went across to the bed and sat down beside her mother. Megan stroked her hair and they smiled complicitly at each other. Then both women turned to look at Adam. Two identical pairs of big, dark eyes stared back at him, their expressions expectant.

Adam felt his cock throb insistently and he grinned.

'Yes, ma'am,' he answered.

Both Megan and Rhiordan smiled happily.

'Come and join us then, honey,' Megan said, patting the edge of the bed, 'it's going to be a long night.'

Adam began to unbutton his shirt.

Chapter Six

THE TWO WOMEN watched him, their eyes so hot as they moved across his flesh Adam could almost feel the sizzling trail left by their gaze as they followed his fingers. His throat felt thick and dry; his heart pounded a slow, steady rhythm that reverberated in his ears, making him feel slightly dizzy.

The air in the room seemed to have thickened and stilled, invisible threads of sexual tension binding the three of them together like silken twine. Adam shrugged his shirt from his shoulders. It fell down each arm, bunching at the wrists where his cuffs were still buttoned.

He tugged each hand through the cuff and let the shirt fall to the floor.

'Mmm – nice bod!' Megan breathed, shifting forward slightly to get a closer look.

Rhiordan giggled. Smiling at Adam, she encouraged him to go on.

'I love that leather belt, Adam,' she said as he began to unbuckle it. 'It's so heavy and *masculine* . . .' She drew out the last word as if she enjoyed the feeling of the syllables rolling on her tongue.

Adam grinned at her and eased the belt with deliberate provocation through each of the belt loops in turn. It made a dull scraping sound as it travelled across the fabric of his trousers before falling to the ground with a dull thud.

Conscious of being watched, he bent down to remove his shoes and socks before starting on his trousers. The sight of him naked but for his footwear would, he knew, be more likely to elicit guffaws of mirth than sighs of rapture, which wasn't what he had in mind. He caught the light of approval in the older woman's eyes as he straightened, and knew he had his 'audience' captivated when he began to unbutton his fly.

The tension in the room seemed to take on a thrilling, expectant quality, as if time was standing still, holding its breath. The sweet scent of female arousal made Adam's penis swell, and he nudged the buttons of his fly through the stiff buttonholes with difficulty. When the task was accomplished he was glad to relieve the pressure, slipping his trousers and boxer shorts down his legs together in one swift movement.

'My, oh my!' Megan breathed as he straightened and she caught sight of his erection for the first time. 'What a fine specimen!'

'Ma!' Rhiordan protested mildly, 'don't! You're embarrassing him!'

Megan glanced briefly at Adam's face before resuming her blatant visual exploration of his cock.

'He doesn't look too embarrassed to me,' she retorted mildly. 'May I?'

For a second, Adam wondered what she meant. He watched quizzically as she slid her body sensuously to the end of the bed. As her feet touched the floor so that she was sitting almost at an eye-level with his crotch, he realised she was actually waiting for his tacit permission before she touched him. As if he was going to refuse!

He smiled. Maybe this was some kind of quaint Welsh custom, a ritual to be performed before things got serious.

'Be my guest,' he said, his pupils dilating as he ran his eyes appreciatively over the voluptuous curve of Megan's breasts, which were almost spilling over the top of the basque.

Her skin was as white as full cream milk, patterned with a delicate-tracery of pale blue veins. The cleft between her breasts was deep and shadowy, and Adam was seized by a vision of himself running the length of his cock along the deep, heated crease . . .

'Aah!' While he had been busy day-dreaming, Megan had reached out and taken him into her hand. Her palm was cool and soft as it ran along the rigid shaft of his cock, and Adam felt his balls kick with delight.

He caught Rhiordan's eye across her mother's head and sucked in his breath. Her big, dark eyes were like two huge, lambent pools, her arousal plain and unashamed. It was clear that it turned her on to watch her lover being caressed by her mother. This was obviously not the first time that mother and daughter had played out this particular scenario – they were progressing with smoothly choreographed precision, perfectly in tune with each other. The thought made Adam shiver.

Sensing the tension that radiated from Rhiordan as she watched, he felt his own excitement move up a gear. Two lovely women, one rock-hard cock, one long night. It seemed to Adam to be the perfect combination.

He swallowed as Megan slid softly to the floor so that she was kneeling in front of him. Her fingers had worked beneath the swollen sacs of his testicles and she probed gently, rolling the distended skin with the pads of her fingertips. Her soft, scarlet-painted lips brushed delicately against the tip of his penis, making him groan out loud.

'That's what you want, Adam, isn't it?' Rhiordan said. 'That's what you like.'

Her voice was low and husky, vibrating with unsuppressed excitement.

'That's what they all like, darling – haven't I always taught you that?'

Megan turned to took at Rhiordan over her shoulder and mother and daughter exchanged a brief, complicit smile.

Adam looked down into Megan's upturned face. It was like looking at a softer, older version of Rhiordan and he was momentarily disorientated. Then Megan smiled wickedly at him, almost as if she could read his mind.

'One thing at a time, lover,' she murmured.

Then, before he could dwell on her words, her soft lips opened wide into a greedy 'o' and she slipped the tip of his penis between them.

A dart of pure pleasure shot through Adam as she slowly drew the length of him into her mouth. It felt as though he was being drawn into a channel of soft, heated velvet. Her mouth enclosed him, concentrating all his attention on the buzz of sensation along his shaft.

Vaguely, he registered her fingers moving beneath his perineum to ease along the crease of his buttocks. Automatically, he tensed, clenching his muscles so that, for a moment, her fingers were trapped.

Megan waited patiently, not forcing anything, concentrating instead on fellating him. Inevitably, he

97

relaxed, leaving her free to continue her insistent caress.

Reaching the tightly closed corona of his anus, she probed gently at the ring of muscle at the entrance before pressing one finger firmly home.

'Aah!' he sighed once more, his legs buckling as she moved her finger in and out of the tight channel of his anus.

He felt her rub against the spot on the inner surface, causing an almost excruciating burst of sensation which made his head swim. Closing his eyes, he rocked on the balls of his feet, thrusting his cock to the back of her throat. He felt it give and found himself buried more deeply in a woman's throat than he had ever been before. Megan seemed to be consuming him, taking him expertly towards the point of no return.

Just as he thought he couldn't hold out any longer, she suddenly withdrew her finger and, moving her head back again, circled the head of his cock twice with her tongue.

He groaned, needing every shred of his self control not to grab her by the back of the head and force her back down on him. Opening his eyes, he saw that she was smiling up at him knowingly, his every thought an open secret, no longer his own. The idea sent a dark thrill of pleasure along his spine.

'Mmm,' she said, sitting back on her heels and looking up at him, 'delicious.'

To his surprise, Adam realised that he was shaking. A few more minutes of that treatment and he would have come, spilling his seed down her accommodating throat. As it was, his cock felt so hard it literally ached.

'Poor Adam!' Rhiordan purred, slipping off the bed and moving to stand behind him. 'It's not nice to tease, Mam – look what it's done to him!'

She reached around him and folded her hand gently over his throbbing shaft. Adam felt as if it would burst. Her soft breasts pressed into his back as she flattened herself against him, moving her hand slowly up and down his cock.

'Rhiordan,' he croaked, 'I—'

'Don't make him come, Rhiordan,' Megan said, cutting across him. 'He'll be no use to us for a good half hour if we let him come now.'

Adam's eyes widened. *Half an hour*? How long did they expect him to go on? He smiled ruefully to himself, acknowledging a small dark thrill at being used by them. He had no problem with being a sex object, if that's what they wanted!

Immediately, Rhiordan let him go, though she still stood next to him, her hands moving to sit proprietorially on his hips. Adam let out an involuntary groan as she rubbed herself against him and he felt the wiry pad of her mons scrape provocatively against his buttocks.

Megan laughed wickedly.

'Patience, my boy,' she told him, rising slowly to her feet. 'Patience has its own reward.'

Adam regarded her through half-closed eyes. Though she was small, no more than five foot two or three, and plump, her figure was a perfectly proportioned hour-glass. Her breasts and hips billowed voluptuously from a waist that was surprisingly narrow and tapered into strong, broad thighs.

The whiteness of her skin fascinated him, and he reached out to run his fingertips across her shoulder and down one arm. She felt like fine satin and he was gripped by the urge to touch her all over, to run his hands, his lips, his tongue across that soft, alabaster skin, seeking out all her secret places.

It seemed, though, that his urges counted for very little in this room this night. With Rhiordan's pliant body pressed tightly against his back and Megan standing so close he could sense the kiss of her warm breath against his throat, Adam felt besieged. It wasn't an unpleasant sensation, and he was quite content to let them use him however they wanted – their pleasure was bound, eventually, to lead to his own.

He held his breath as Megan came nearer. Watching his face closely, she moved to stand in front of him, not quite touching, but close enough for him to feel the heat of her skin radiating out towards him.

Suddenly, it was difficult to breathe. Sandwiched between the two women, he felt engulfed by femininity: the warmth and softness of their flesh, the scent of their skin, their perfume . . . their sex. *Oh, their sex . . .*

His cock throbbed with an intensity close to pain. It formed a rigid, inflexible barrier between him and the older woman as she pressed herself against him. Adam sighed as it sank into the cushiony softness of her belly, and then her arms were around his neck and she was kissing him.

Her mouth and tongue tasted of wine and honey, the sweetest nectar. Meanwhile, Rhiordan was undulating softly against his back, rubbing herself against him like a cat. Adam reached behind him to stroke the soft skin of her flank. The shiver this invoked echoed in the pit of his belly. He felt a tightening in his chest and the boiling throb that normally signalled he was about to come.

As if sensing this, Megan stopped kissing him and Rhiordan moved away. Adam felt bereft; the air now surrounding him seemed cold and unfriendly and he pulled back from the brink. Megan's smile was almost kindly.

'Come and lie down,' she said.

Adam needed no second bidding. The bed dipped under his weight as he sat down, sliding along to the pillow end on his bottom so that he didn't have to take his eyes off the two women. Rhiordan smiled happily at him and began to strip off the baby-doll outfit she had been wearing. As her familiar body came into full view, Adam felt his cock twitch with remembered joy.

Then it was Megan's turn. A fizz of anticipation sparked through Adam as she hooked her thumb beneath one strap of her basque and ran it thoughtfully up and down. The basque was front-fastening, dozens of tiny hooks and eyes running from the middle of her breasts to the point just above her pubic mound, where the soft fur of her mons began.

Adam imagined slipping each hook through each eye, one by one, slowly revealing her luscious, naked body . . .

'Come here,' Megan said, her voice low and caressing. 'Unhook me.'

Convinced now that she could read his mind, Adam slid back down the bed so that he was sitting in front of her, in the same position she had adopted when she asked if it was all right to touch him.

He wished she'd touch him now! Every square centimetre of his skin seemed to tingle with anticipation, every nerve-ending acutely aware of this lovely, confident, mature woman who was now waiting patiently for him to undress her.

His fingers shook as he reached for the top hook. It slipped easily through the dainty little eye, encouraging him. As if to torment him, Rhiordan reached between him and her mother and began to stroke his iron-hard shaft, not firmly enough to stimulate him beyond control, but lightly, sending shivers up and down his spine.

'Careful,' Megan whispered, but Rhiordan seemed not to hear her, continuing to stroke rhythmically up and down, up and down. It was maddening, yet Adam knew he didn't want her to stop, any more than he wanted to stop unfastening Megan's basque.

As he reached the top of her waist, her large, squashy breasts spilled out of the opening into his waiting hands.

'Oh . . . mmm . . .' he murmured, incoherent with pleasure as he cupped them and buried his face deep in the fragrant channel they formed. Meanwhile, he continued to unfasten each hook and eye, eager now to have her naked.

The basque peeled away from her body, revealing her to him. Slowly, Adam traced the red lines on her skin caused by the constriction, his tongue soothing. The plump folds of her belly were smooth and white, the crisp, dark curls over her mons shockingly black against the paleness of her skin.

The elasticated welts of her stockings gripped her upper thighs, close to her crotch, accentuating the dark triangle of hair which was at Adam's eye level. He could smell her arousal, a heavy scent that made his head spin.

Glancing up at her face, he saw she was watching him through narrowed eyes, her breathing quick and shallow. Encouraged by the physical signs of her approval, he placed his thumbs on either side of her sex lips and gently peeled them apart.

Her inner labia were moist and smooth, suffused with blood. He could see her clitoris pulsing at their apex, beating a powerful tattoo of desire.

Slowly, determined not to rush it, he leaned forward and touched the very tip of his tongue against the shiny bud.

'Oh, yes . . . yes . . .'

Megan seemed to lose her balance and she reached out to steady herself by placing her hands on his shoulders. As if inebriated by the sight, sound and taste of her arousal, Adam thrust his tongue along the grooves of her sex, seeking out every tiny, sensitive spot, burrowing into the hot, wet entrance to her body.

Adam wanted to drown in the copious juices within. The dewy moisture smeared his lips and chin and nose, and still he pressed on, driving Megan to the point of climax.

He knew the second she tipped over the edge. Her clitoris seemed to stiffen for an instant, then it throbbed fiercely against his tongue, and a fresh gush of fluid bathed his face.

'Don't stop . . . don't stop!' Megan screeched, grinding her hips against him until he could no longer breathe. Just as he thought he might suffocate, she almost toppled backwards, staggering away from him on unsteady legs.

Adam reached for her and guided her gently down on to the bed beside him. Putting an arm protectively around her shoulder, he kissed her full on the mouth, drawing the sweetness from it, relishing its heat.

'My turn!' Rhiordan demanded, climbing on to his lap so that she was straddling his cock.

It fitted neatly into the deep crease of her bottom, the tip nosing its way as if with a life of its own towards her sex.

'No, not yet,' she commanded, wriggling about so that the desired destination eluded him, 'I want you to frig me.'

Adam allowed himself a rueful grin. 'God save me from bossy women,' he said.

Rhiordan arched an eyebrow. 'Oh really?' she said.

He laughed. 'No, not really,' he admitted, slipping his fingers into the hot, dripping channel of her sex.

Adam had never known her to be so wet. Her clitoris was swollen to the size of a small cherry, the centre as hard as a pip. He knew it wouldn't take long for her to reach a climax, then maybe it would be *his* turn. Hell, he needed it! His balls felt taut and uncomfortable, fit to burst while his cock . . . he could not find the words to describe the tension contained in that central rod of flesh. Just thinking about it made him moan softly.

Dipping his head, he lifted one of Rhiordan's large, ripe nipples to his lips and gorged himself on it.

'Oh, that's good – suck it harder!' she cried, moving her hips frantically back and forth on his fingers. 'Harder . . . bite it . . . suck it . . . oh . . . oh . . . I'm coming!'

As her daughter squirmed in ecstasy on Adam's lap, Megan leaned across and kissed him on the mouth, thrusting her tongue against his and pressing her breasts against the side of his body.

Adam knew he couldn't stand this level of provocation for much longer. It was time to reassert himself, to take control. With a muted roar, he tipped Rhiordan off his lap and flipped her on to her stomach on the bed. Laughing, Megan joined them, thrusting her hips up into the air and waggling her bottom temptingly at him.

Lifting Rhiordan's hips to the same level as her mother's, Adam looked from one to the other, breathing heavily. The sight confronting him was enough to make the blood roar in his ears and it took a tremendous act of willpower to hold back, to wait still longer.

Two pairs of plump, rounded buttocks, two moist,

red purses hanging like ripe fruits between, each open for him, inviting him to plunge in . . .

'Stay still,' he barked, his innate desire to be in control taking over.

The surge of power went to his head. He felt ten feet tall, invincible. Taking full advantage of the element of surprise, he brought down both hands at once and delivered an open-handed slap to both bottoms.

Rhiordan and Megan squealed as their flesh trembled and shook.

'Adam—' Rhiordan began.

'Quiet!' he said, spanking her again.

'What about me?' Megan turned to look at him over her shoulder, her expression mock-petulant.

'I said stay still,' Adam hissed, slapping her again.

There was something powerfully erotic about the sound of flesh against flesh and the way the women's bottoms quivered and shook. Though they both moaned and squealed, they pushed their buttocks higher, eager for the contact of his hand. After half a dozen more light, open-handed slaps, their bottoms glowed pink and both were moaning softly, faces pressed tightly into the pillows, muffling their cries.

Breathless, Adam paused to catch his breath.

'Are you going to stay still now?' he said, his voice low and silky.

Two muffled 'yeses' came from the pillows and he smiled to himself. Two women, bottoms raised, legs apart, ready and waiting for him. A living fantasy. He would have defied any man to hold out any longer.

Slowly, relishing every minute, he positioned himself carefully before sinking his cock into Rhiordan's hot, familiar body. The air came out of him in a long, satisfied sigh as he felt her silky inner flesh enclose him. If he hadn't been stimulated to the point of madness he felt he could have stayed there, happily buried in her body, simply relishing the way her muscles clenched rhythmically around him.

But glancing at Megan he saw that she was waiting for him, still in the same position, lovely bottom held high, her impatience barely concealed. Reaching across, he slipped his hand between her thighs and caressed the swollen folds of her labia, marvelling at how wet and hot she was. He had to have her too.

Rhiordan moaned in protest as he withdrew from her. Sinking into Megan's waiting sex, Adam marvelled at how different she felt from her daughter. Just as beautiful, but different. Not as tight, but softer, her innermost flesh hot and melting against the intrusion of his cock.

Once, twice, he thrust in and out of her before returning to Rhiordan. He couldn't keep it up for long. Moving from one woman to the other once more, he was frenzied, out of control. A powerful, white-hot wave of sensation rolled through him as he felt himself reach the brink, beads of sweat breaking through every pore, bathing him in a fine layer of moisture.

He barely knew who he was inside as he threw back his head and roared, feeling the seed pumping gloriously along his shaft, bursting from him in powerful jags, making his head swim and his heart pound.

It was mind-blowing, an orgasm that went on and on, until he felt he couldn't have anything more left in him. He slumped over the back of the woman beneath him, feeling a second body rubbing against his side, prolonging his pleasure. The room was silent save for the sounds of ragged breathing, the smell of sex hanging heavily in the air, enclosing them all in a sensual post-coital fog, binding them together.

Adam didn't know how long it took for his heart rate to slow and his breathing to normalise. Vaguely, he was aware of gentle arms guiding him to lie down, of his cheek sinking on to a soft, pillowy bosom. He felt drained, exhilarated, yet totally at peace. Most of all he was very, very sleepy.

'That's right, honey,' said Megan – or was it Rhiordan? – softly against his hair. 'You sleep now and gather your strength. It's going to be a long, long night . . .'

He murmured, half in protest, half in agreement, but he was already drifting away, surrounded in a cocoon of soft, naked female flesh.

Susie couldn't sleep. The thought of Sebastian lying alone in the guest bedroom, so close, yet so far away made her hot and restless. She barely understood the feelings he had awoken in her with his rough caresses: they weren't what she had expected sexual arousal to be about. Yet that was undoubtedly what she had experienced – was still experiencing – and she could not settle.

Adam hadn't returned home yet. The bedside clock showed three a.m. and still she hadn't heard the wheels of his car on the gravel outside. Not that she was waiting to hear him come home. There was no question about how *his* evening had ended.

Though she knew it was unreasonable, Susie felt curiously betrayed. Her new 'brother' and her best friend – their passion for each other made her feel excluded.

Unwelcome images crowded into her mind of Adam and Rhiordan in bed together. Moving restlessly in her lonely single bed, she told herself it was only because of the way she felt about Sebastian that caused her to feel so agitated.

Slowly, almost absent-mindedly, she slipped her fingers between her thighs. To her surprise, her sex felt hot and swollen, the surface slicked with moisture.

Glowing sensations ran through her as she stroked herself gently. Did she really want Sebastian to touch her like this . . . and more? She replayed the scene as they came into the garden in her mind, closing her eyes and concentrating on the gentle pleasures radiating out from her clitoris as she caressed herself.

Gently, almost reverently, she moved the distended little bud against the pubic bone, rolling it back and forth until she gasped, little sparks of sensation shooting through her body, making her feel hot and shivery all at once.

It was a gentle climax which left her feeling, if anything, even more restless and unsatisfied. Whimpering softly into the darkness, she squeezed her thighs tightly together, trapping her hand against her sex, trying to prolong the muted waves of orgasm. It was no use. For Susie was aware that, even as she came, the face that accompanied her over the brink was not Sebastian's, but Adam's.

It came to her then, in a rare flash of self-knowledge, that the feeling she had when she thought of Rhiordan with Adam was simple jealousy. Infuriating though she found him, somehow she had managed to fall in love with Adam Corcoran. It was *him* she wanted in bed beside her, *his* lips against her breasts, *his* hand replacing hers in the most intimate of caresses . . .

'No!' she whispered into the forgiving darkness. 'Not Adam. It's Sebastian I want.'

She forced herself to think of the other man, fiercely

visualising her new life in London and the part that Sebastian would play in it. She was going to be rich and famous, achieve everything she had always wanted.

To her, Sebastian represented the lifestyle she yearned for: he was cosmopolitan, sophisticated, smooth and urbane. Sexy though he was, Adam would always be a farm boy at heart.

What's wrong with that? a small, mischievous voice whispered in her head. 'Plenty!' she said aloud, angry that the thought had entered her mind. She could have Sebastian, if she wanted; she could never have Adam. Not if she wanted London and all it represented.

Susie always got what she wanted. Not to do so was unthinkable. So, she told herself, she would learn to want what she *could* have, then illicit thoughts of Adam would go away. They had to go away! She'd dreamt of this chance Sebastian was giving her ever since she was a little girl and was chosen as the village May Queen. She wasn't going to let her foolish heart ruin her life. No way!

Closing her eyes, she willed herself to sleep. A gentle post-orgasmic heat enfolded her, lulling her towards oblivion and dreams . . . of Adam.

Chapter Seven

'*I DON'T CARE* what you say – I'm going to London and you can't stop me!' Susie glared at Diana and Jack, conscious of Adam still lingering at the dinner table, saying nothing, but taking everything in with that lazy, half amused expression of his that she found so infuriating.

Diana ran her fingers through her hair, disturbing its usual neatness in her agitation.

'All we're trying to say is—'

'All you're trying to say, Mum, is that you took a dislike to Sebastian – God knows why, he was pleasant enough – and are using him as an excuse to stop me from going away. Well, I'm telling you, you can forget it! It's not going to work!'

'Listen to your mother, Susie,' Jack interjected quietly. 'She only has your interests at heart.'

Susie snorted her disbelief. It wasn't fair! Conscious that she was close to angry tears, she bit her lip and scowled. Diana took advantage of her momentary silence.

'Mr Semple is probably a very good photographer, we're not questioning that at this point. Whatever you might think, this is not about him. What we are saying is that we know too little about where you'll be living and who you'll have to turn to if you're homesick, or—'

'I am not a child!' Susie burst out, stamping her foot on the quarry-tiled floor.

'Then stop behaving like one and listen to reason,' Jack snapped.

Jack was normally so easy-going that he never snapped at anyone, least of all Susie, whom he had always treated with a kind of affectionate, amused tolerance. For a moment the shock of being spoken to sharply by him kept her quiet. Gradually, though, annoyance at his nerve took over. Who the hell did he think he was? She would not have Jack Corcoran thinking he could tell her what to do and what not to do. Pointedly ignoring him, Susie squared up to her mother.

'It's not reasonable just because it's what *you* think. And I'm not a fool. I know this is about Sebastian. Now, I'm sorry you didn't like him, but you have to admit that it was good of him to come all this way to meet you. He didn't have to do that, but the fact that he did must tell you something good about him! If you can't see it, Mummy, then you have to be the most suspicious mother in the world!'

'Susie . . .'

'No, Mum, I'm sorry. I would rather you gave your blessing to what I want to do, of course I would. But the fact that you won't isn't going to stop me from doing it. So I'm going to London tomorrow as planned, whether you like it or not, and nothing you or anybody else can say will stop me.'

She marched out of the dining room, her head held high, trying desperately to prove that she was as mature and responsible as she needed to be.

111

Behind her, she left frustration and despair. Jack regarded his wife's anguished expression and sighed.

'She's right, Diana, we can't stop her.'

'But that man, Jack, the way he looked at her ... Ugh!' Diana shuddered. 'You said yourself you didn't like the look of him, and yet I'm expected to entrust my daughter to his care without question.'

'Susie is old enough to decide for herself now,' Jack reminded her gently.

Diana shook her head vigorously. 'I know she's of age, but in many ways she's dreadfully immature.' She clenched her fists as she spoke, creasing her forehead into a deep frown. 'Oh, Jack, I hate to think of her all alone in a big city. She's so vulnerable!'

Adam said nothing, but privately agreed with Diana. She might be a big shot in the local village, but amongst the likes of Sebastian Semple, Susie would be eaten alive.

'Hard as it is, you have to allow her to make her own mistakes, honey,' Jack was saying, sliding his arm around his wife's shoulders. 'It's one of the hardest bits about being a parent – letting them go. You can't wrap her in cotton wool and keep her close forever. She'd be bound to rebel in the end.'

'I know that, Jack. But there are some mistakes that young people can't afford to make at all. She's not going to London tomorrow, we have to find a way to stop her.'

Diana rose and, stacking a few plates haphazardly, went to the kitchen, leaving Jack and Adam alone.

'What do you think?' Jack asked his son after a few minutes.

Adam glanced up in surprise. 'Me? It's not my business.'

'I asked you what you *thought*, dammit! Do you think

you can live in a family and not be involved with what goes on from day to day?'

'Okay,' Adam said, taken aback by Jack's outburst. 'Okay, for what it's worth, I'll tell you what I think. I think that Susie is heading for a fall, but unlike Diana, I don't think that's necessarily such a bad thing.'

'What do you mean?'

Adam shrugged. 'The girl's got a lot of growing up to do. A dose of real life won't do her any harm. And if it all gets too much for her, she can always run home to Mummy, can't she?'

Jack stared at him. 'Don't you care?'

Adam stared right back. 'Not much,' he said eventually, wondering why he felt it necessary to lie.

The two men stared at each other for a long moment. Jack's expression was bleak and Adam was surprised to find he actually cared what his father thought of him. And he didn't like being found wanting.

The argument continued over breakfast the following morning, with Diana becoming more and more desperate. Eventually, she lost her temper.

'I don't want to come the heavy-handed parent, Susie, but you leave me no choice. You might think you're old enough to know what's best for you, but the way you're behaving now only goes to prove that you don't. Far from it, in fact.' She fixed Susie with a cool, unwavering gaze. 'You will do as you are told.'

Susie faced her mother across the table, two hectic spots of colour on her cheeks, eyes bright with unshed tears.

'I won't, Mummy, not this time. I know why you're so keen to stop me anyway,' she added bitterly.

'What do you mean?'

Susie shrugged slightly, as if what she was about to say didn't matter. The sudden tension around the table proved that she fooled no one.

'When I go to London I'll be out of the way, won't I?'

'What's that supposed to mean? Out of whose way?' Diana could hear herself growing shrill but couldn't control the note of panic creeping into her voice.

'You and Jack'll be free then to get on with your lives without any reminders of Dad—'

'Susie!' Jack said warningly as he saw the look of shock on Diana's face, but there was no stopping her now she had begun. A dam had burst, letting out a torrent of harsh, hurting words.

'You drove him away, didn't you? Well, you haven't got to do that to me – I'm going of my own accord!'

Diana had turned white and she clutched the back of her chair for support as she faced her angry daughter.

'How can you say such things! You don't know the half of it, Susie, you were only a little girl . . .'

'I was old enough to know you made my daddy run away. You didn't even let him say goodbye!' Her voice dropped to a whisper; even she was shocked by what she had said. 'I'll never forgive you for that.'

Diana's mouth opened and closed, but no sound came out. Tears streaked Susie's cheeks now, but she didn't move, just stared at her mother with a mixture of contrition and defiance. Finally, Diana found her voice.

'We'll talk about this later,' she said shakily. 'But in the meantime, you are *not* going to London, and that's final.'

'Yes, I am. I'm going right now, in fact, I'll catch the morning train instead of the afternoon one. And you'd better not try to stop me.'

She ran out of the room, leaving Diana, Jack and

Adam staring after her in shocked silence.

'I never dreamt she blamed me for Peter's departure,' Diana said after a few moments.

'I'm sure she doesn't – it was just anger talking,' Jack soothed her, putting his arm around her shoulders. 'Adam – go see if you can talk some sense into her.'

It was the last thing Adam wanted to do, but seeing a chance to redeem himself after disappointing Jack the night before, he reluctantly followed Susie up the stairs.

She was in her bedroom, flinging clothes into a suitcase. Adam leaned against the doorjamb and watched her in silence for a few minutes. Her colour was high and her eyes glowed like blue ice. Her hair was dishevelled and tear tracks streaked the fine-textured amber skin of her cheeks.

For once Susie did not appear to be conscious of how she looked, or how her appearance might be affecting those around her. Adam wondered if she realised how much more beautiful she looked when she was acting naturally rather than posing. Somehow he doubted it.

'You're off, then,' he said conversationally.

'What does it look like?' She glanced up for long enough to scowl at him, then her eyes narrowed. 'What do you want?'

Adam held up his hands. 'Hey, back off! I was only going to see if I could help.'

'I don't need your help,' Susie muttered, struggling with the zip on her bulging case.

Adam watched her for a few moments before casually stepping forward and fastening it for her. As he stood beside her, he was suddenly conscious of the faint scent of the shampoo she had used that morning and he felt his senses tingle.

'Thank you,' she said grudgingly, the stiffness in her

tone making him wonder if she felt it too, this inexplicable attraction.

'You see – I can be useful,' he said softly, unable to keep the low, sensual note from creeping into his voice. 'Is there anything else I can help with?'

Susie seemed to shiver slightly, then she moved abruptly away from him. 'There's nothing, thank you.'

'Not even a lift to the station?' Adam doubted whether that was quite the kind of help Jack had had in mind when he sent him up here, but for the moment it was all he could think of. At least he could report back to Diana that Susie had caught her train safely.

'Well?' he prompted when she didn't reply.

He could see she was wavering, torn between not wanting to have to accept help from him, and needing a lift.

'All right,' she said at last, her blue eyes blazing as she caught his eye.

He grinned. 'I'm honoured,' he muttered as he picked her case up off the bed.

Adam carried her case downstairs and loaded it into the car. He watched from outside as Susie said a stiff goodbye to a distraught Diana, offering Jack no more than a formal nod. Catching his father's eye over her head, Adam could see that Jack was faintly bewildered by the fact that, far from persuading her to stay, he was driving her to the station, and he guessed he would have some explaining to do later.

Tension emanated from her every pore as Susie climbed into the car beside him.

'Sure you don't want to think about this some more?' Adam asked her.

'Just drive.' Susie snapped.

He waited until she had made herself comfortable

and had fastened her seat belt before drawing away.

'So, the great adventure begins, does it?' he said after several minutes of stony silence.

Susie's brief glare scorched him. 'What's it got to do with you?'

He shrugged. 'Not a lot. Just making conversation.'

She was quiet for a moment, then the words seemed to burst out of her, taking on a life of their own. 'I should have thought that you'd be cheering, now I'm on my way.'

'Yeah? How so?'

'Oh, come on, Adam – you were quick enough to offer to drive me to the station. Admit it – you can't wait to see the back of me, can you?'

Stunned by her vehemence, Adam merely shook his head in disbelief.

'Huh! I knew it! You couldn't wait for me to go so that you can get on with playing happy families with your father and *my* mother, on *my father's* farm. You Corcorans – you're all the same. You – aah!'

She cried out as Adam slewed the car to a halt at the side of the road. As he killed the engine and turned to face her, he saw the brief chill of fear that crossed her face, but chose to ignore it, matching her glare for glare.

'Just who the hell do you think you are?' he grated, allowing his fury to show.

'Start this car up again at once! I—'

'Don't give me orders, Susie Jones! Unlike your friends I'm not impressed by you and, unlike your poor mother, I can't be hurt by your selfish ranting.'

'How dare you!'

'Oh, I dare all right, sweetheart. I happen to like your mother and the way you spoke to her back there was disgraceful. She didn't deserve it.'

117

The fact that the same thought had already crossed her own mind did not lessen Susie's outrage; if anything, it intensified it, turning guilt into righteous anger.

'I don't have to listen to this! Open the boot and I'll get my bag.'

'Yeah? And drag it two miles to the station?'

'If I have to! What are you doing—Adam! Unlock the doors this instant!'

Susie pumped the door handle, only to find that Adam had activated the central locking and she was trapped inside the car with him. Sheer fury made her strike out at him, but his reflexes were too fast. His hand shot out and intercepted hers and with a swift tug he pulled her sharply against him.

'Oh!' she gasped.

She wriggled frantically against his grasp, telling herself it was because the gear stick was pressing painfully into her ribs, not wanting to admit, even silently, that his nearness thrilled her. It was all she could do not to cry out with contrary disappointment when he pushed her away.

'You are the limit!' he spat as he restarted the engine. 'Go to London – London is welcome to you! Maybe after a few months amongst strangers you'll lose that gigantic chip from your shoulder and start to appreciate the family that loves you.'

The family that loves you? Did Adam include himself in that equation? she wondered miserably.

The car screeched to a halt outside the small local station and Adam unlocked the doors and turned to look at her. Susie had never felt more wretched in her life. Silently, she climbed out of the car and went to fetch her suitcase from the boot. Adam climbed out of the driver's seat and watched her, his expression no longer thunderous, but inscrutable.

Drawing level with him, Susie paused. Part of her wanted to turn and run, but another, far stronger part of her wanted to make things right with Adam before she left.

'Let's not say goodbye like this,' she pleaded.

Adam made an indecipherable sound at the back of his throat and the next thing she knew she was against his chest and his arms were around her body. Wordlessly, she raised her face to his. Any murmurs of protest she might half-heartedly have uttered were swallowed up by his kiss.

Susie thought she had been kissed before, but nothing had prepared her for this. Adam's lips were hard and demanding, yet strangely tender as they moved over hers, coaxing her to part them and grant him access to the heat of her mouth.

At first she stood still, too stunned to react. For a microsecond, she hovered on the verge of outrage, but it was not truly an emotion she felt. Suddenly, there seemed to be a softening, an actual physical surrender which took her over, making her melt into his arms, sending her own up to twine around his neck, and her mouth opened sweetly under his.

Sensing her capitulation, Adam kissed her more deeply, meeting her tremulous tongue with his, pressing her tightly against him. A small part of her mind, the part that was still coherent, recognised how well they fitted together, hip to hip, breast to chest, almost as if they were two matching halves of one whole, made to complement each other.

Clinging to him, she revelled in the sensation of rightness that accompanied the blossoming of their

119

mutual desire. Adam pressed her closer so that she could feel the wholly masculine hardening of his body against the softness of hers.

It was this stark evidence of his physical arousal that made her draw back, pulling away from him with a small cry of anguish. It was too much, too soon, and at the wrong time.

Putting a stop to it when it had barely begun was the hardest thing Susie had ever had to do, but she knew it was necessary for her own survival, not only to stop it, but to forget that it had ever happened at all.

For a second they stared at each other, suspended in time. Adam could read the anguish in her over-bright eyes, and knew his own feelings were reflected there.

'Susie—' he began, but just then the sound of the early train approaching distracted them, making them both turn to look towards the platform.

'I . . . I have to go,' she choked.

'Wait—'

'I have to . . . goodbye . . .'

Susie heaved her suitcase up and ran awkwardly to the ticket office.

Adam watched her go. He had been as surprised by what had happened as she had been. It might well have made everything even more complicated, but he couldn't bring himself to regret it. As he stood and watched her disappear behind the railings, he could still taste the sweetness of her lips, still feel the womanly imprint of her body against his and he knew he wasn't going to be able to forget in a hurry. He knew she was inexperienced, but there was no doubt in his mind that Susie was teetering on the brink of womanhood, ripe for love.

He turned away and climbed back into the car,

unable to shake off the feeling of regret that he would not be the one to teach her. Turning the key in the ignition, his fists clenched as he thought of Sebastian Semple and the way the man's eyes had roamed proprietorially over Susie's body, as if he already owned her. And Susie didn't even seem to realise, she was so blinded by her own ambition, blinkered by vanity!

As he drove away, Adam could not get the thought out of his mind that that man was waiting for her in London, thinking she was a ripe fruit just waiting to be plucked. And he had let her walk away, without so much as a warning!

Suddenly, Adam was seized by such a sense of urgency, he felt compelled to turn back, to stop her. He had to know if she had been as affected by the kiss they had shared as he had. If she had, then surely she would stay and they would work things out?

Galvanised into action, he executed a three-point turn in the middle of the road and turned back towards the station. Bringing the car to a halt, he killed the engine and jumped out.

The moment he reached the barrier and saw the train pulling away, he realised it was too late.

'Will you be wanting a platform ticket?' the Irish guard asked him.

'Yeah – how much?'

The guard shook his head and waved him through. 'Get on with you.'

Adam ran on to the platform, his eyes scanning the passengers seated at the windows. She was sitting near the back, staring out of the window. He raised his hand.

'Susie!'

She looked up as the train rolled slowly past him.

'Adam?'

She pressed her palm against the window, her eyes questioning as he walked alongside the train as it slowly gathered speed.

'Call home when you get there!' he shouted, but couldn't be sure she heard him, for she frowned, her eyes hanging on to his until the last possible moment, as he ran out of platform and was forced to stop.

Susie arrived on Paddington station feeling tired and dishevelled. She hadn't been able to get Adam out of her mind all the way from Wales. Why had he kissed her like that? More intriguing still, what had he been trying to say on the platform?

Coming so soon after the row with her mother, what had happened between her and Adam was too much. It was bad enough to have left with ill feeling between herself and Diana; they had always been so close, and as Susie had only been half aware of the feelings she harboured about her father's disappearance, her outburst that morning had come as almost as much of a surprise to her as it had to Diana.

As for Adam . . . she shook her head, trying to clear her thoughts. It was nothing more than a fleeting attack of lust, she told herself stoutly. After all, Adam was involved with Rhiordan.

Thinking of Rhiordan confused her even further. She had left without saying goodbye to her best friend, and that saddened her. It was as if she had severed all her links with home and childhood in one fell swoop. Burnt all her boats so that London *had* to work out. There was no going back.

Because she had taken an earlier train, there was no one to meet her and, already feeling homesick for her small Welsh community, she felt overwhelmed by the noise and the crush of people.

Pull yourself together! she scolded herself silently. It was merely a matter of acclimatisation. Pushing away the uncomfortable thought that the city was unwelcoming rather than exciting, she found a quiet corner on the concourse and rummaged around in her bag for the address Sebastian had given her.

The taxi driver who finally responded to her increasingly frantic signals was taciturn as he drove her through the city streets. So much for the chirpy cockney commentary she had imagined was the cabbies' stock in trade!

Susie gazed out on to the grey, rain-washed pavements, heaving with the afternoon crowds, and her heart sank. In all the time she had dreamed of this moment, she had never imagined she would feel so alone amongst so many people.

They passed a few of the landmarks she had read about and her spirits lifted a little, a small spasm of excitement beginning to tighten in her stomach. She was here, she had actually done it – she'd left home!

Susie smiled and hugged her bag to her. She wouldn't have felt so lost and alone when she arrived if not for the unsettling incident with Adam at the station. His kiss – or, more truthfully, her reaction to it – had confused her, made her forget for a moment her purpose in going away. That, and the row with Diana.

Her smile faded as she thought of the way she had left her mother. She hadn't meant to say the things she had, they'd just sprung from her lips in the heat of the moment. She wasn't even sure she believed half of them.

The realisation was not a happy one, and Susie deliberately pushed away all thoughts of home and Diana and Adam. There was no time for regrets. She couldn't afford to look back, only forwards.

This was the future – her future – and she was determined to make the most of every minute.

Chapter Eight

WHEN THE TAXI driver drew up outside the dingy block of flats, Susie thought he must have made a mistake.

'This can't be it,' she told him, gazing up at the crumbling concrete tower.

'It's the address you gave me,' he insisted, pointing out the graffiti-smeared sign on the wall.

Dismayed, Susie paid him a sum that made her gasp, alarmed at how her limited resources were depleted. Feeling even more miserable, she watched as he drove away, leaving her standing with her suitcase on the pavement.

It was dull and wet and Susie was conscious of a group of youths eyeing her speculatively from where they lounged at the entrance to the flats. Pulling out the piece of paper Sebastian had given her the day before, she re-read the address, even though she knew that the driver had been right. This was the building.

'Lost, are ya?'

Susie whirled round to find one of the youths from the flats addressing her.

'No, thank you, I—'

'Gis a look.' He snatched the piece of paper from her

hand and squinted at the address written on it. Susie became aware of four or five others circling her and cold fear gripped her. They were all younger than her, no more than children, but their dress, their manner and the way they spread out and surrounded her was intimidating.

'Give me that back,' she said, trying to sound firm and authoritative and, she was convinced by the wide grin with which he responded, failing miserably.

'Hey, she wants *Seb-as-ti-an*,' the first youth sang out as he handed her the piece of paper.

'Yo one o' Sebastian's girls?' a dark-skinned boy who looked no older than twelve asked her.

'No ... I mean ... yes,' she said, wondering if he meant one of Sebastian's models.

'You do look like one,' a third told her.

Susie smiled, feeling flattered. 'I look like a model?'

They all fell about laughing, confusing her. 'Yeah – jus' like a *mo-del*,' the first youth answered. 'We'll give you a hand with your bag.'

'Thank you, but—'

'No problem.'

Susie found herself swept along to the doorway of the flats and up the stairs. The stairwell stank of rotting garbage and cat's pee and Susie breathed shallowly through her nose as they all trooped up the stairs.

'Can't we use the lift?' she gasped as they reached the fifth floor.

'S'broke,' one of the youths answered her shortly.

'Only anuvver six floors,' a voice behind her said.

Susie glanced back and realised that the five boys who had elected to walk behind her had done so for a purpose: they were all ogling her bottom as she walked up the stairs.

It was a relief to reach Sebastian's floor, for more reasons than one.

'This is it,' the youth who had carried her bag said, dumping it on the floor outside Sebastian's door. 'Good luck, sister.'

'Oh – wait!' Susie was surprised by the speed with which they disappeared, leaving her alone. She might have felt threatened by them before, but now they had gone she felt exposed in a hostile environment, vulnerable in a way she definitely did not like. From perceiving the boys as a threat, she had almost come, during the progress of their procession up the stairs, to regard them as her protectors.

She hesitated before knocking on the door in front of her. The blue paint was peeling to reveal a yellowed cream colour beneath, and the letterbox lurched drunkenly, held to the door by its two remaining screws. She could hear the rhythmic thump of a loud bass line coming from inside, dance music seeping round the edges of the door and out into the corridor.

When she had pictured Sebastian's studio, Susie had imagined the kind of place that wedding photographers had in Cardiff, only swisher, maybe situated in the West End. Never in her wildest dreams – or her darkest nightmares – had she expected to find him in a crumbling towerblock in an obscure inner-city district she had never even heard of.

Tentatively, Susie touched her knuckles against the door, then rapped them hard, twice. There was definitely movement inside the flat, and she heard the music being turned down slightly as footsteps approached.

The door opened no more than a crack.

'Er . . . hello? I'm looking for Sebastian. He . . . is expecting me today . . .'

'Susie?'

The door opened wider to show Sebastian himself framed in the doorway. His skin looked flushed, his hair dishevelled and his white shirt had come adrift from his trousers, making him look as though he had just rolled out of bed. But all that Susie really took in was the fact that he didn't look best pleased to see her.

'Susie! I wasn't expecting you until six o'clock this afternoon. I was going to meet you at the station. Isn't that what we arranged?' He frowned, trying to remember.

'I know, I . . . You see, there was a change of plan and . . . well, here I am!' She shrugged and gazed up at him, willing him to look at least a little pleased to see her. 'I hope it's all right, just turning up like this?' she added tentatively.

After the initial shock of seeing her standing on his doorstep had worn off, Sebastian seemed to recover himself a little and he smiled.

'Sure, sure it is – I was a bit taken aback, that's all. I was in the middle of a photo shoot, so I wasn't quite with it when I opened the door. Artistic temperament and all that, y'know?' He grinned disarmingly. 'Wait here a minute.'

He closed the door and left her standing in the corridor, feeling awkward. She heard voices coming from inside the flat and a muffled curse as something was knocked over. After a few moments, Sebastian opened the door again and, this time, invited her inside.

Beyond the narrow hallway, a door stood open, leading into a living area. Susie blinked, trying to see into the dim interior.

'Sorry about the light – I've blacked out the windows so that I can control the lighting for each shot.'

'I see,' Susie said faintly, eyeing the makeshift platform in the centre of the room which had been draped with fake fur fabric. 'Who is today's shoot for?'

'What? Oh, I see. Er . . . *Vogue* are interested in this one,' he told her, busying himself with packing away his cameras.

Susie looked around, her gaze taking in the video cameras sited at the four corners of the platform. A niggle of unease made her frown.

'Do you work on spec like that a lot?' she asked innocently.

'How do you mean?'

'Well, I would have thought that a magazine like *Vogue* would commission its photographs.'

Sebastian stood up. 'That shows how little you know, sweetheart, doesn't it?' he said coolly.

Susie waited while he finished packing his equipment away, unsure what to do, but feeling horribly uncomfortable. She didn't recognise this cool, dismissive stranger and she felt she was way out of her depth.

'What's wrong?' he asked her, so suddenly that it didn't occur to her to dissemble.

'This isn't quite what I expected,' she admitted with a nervous laugh.

'What isn't?'

'Your . . . studio.'

Sebastian laughed, dismissing her observation. 'I suppose you expected a glamorous address, lots of glass and chrome?' he said.

'Well . . .' Put like that, Susie felt her expectations sounded foolish.

'Lots of photographers utilise these old flats – saves on overheads.'

'I see,' she replied faintly. Part of her didn't believe

him, but the greater part of her wanted to so desperately. After all, she reasoned with herself, what else could she do but trust him? The only alternative was to go home with her tail between her legs, admitting she was wrong about her ability to cope alone in the city. She simply *couldn't* do that, not after all that she had said. The very idea filled her with horror.

It was that thought that put the steel in her spine and the sparkle in her smile.

'That's better,' Sebastian said. 'For a moment there I thought I must have imagined the star quality I saw in the valleys!'

He patted her bottom encouragingly as he passed her, calling out, 'Holly! Holly, get a move on! I need you to show Susie to the flat!'

'Who's Holly?' Susie asked him.

'One of your new colleagues. You'll like her – she's a good girl. She'll keep an eye on you.'

Susie turned as someone else entered the room.

'Holly, this is Susie, the girl I was telling you about.'

'Hi!'

'Hello.'

Susie stared at the tall, leggy girl who had entered the room. She was wearing a tight black top which clung to the pert contours of her breasts, and a mock leopard-skin skirt no wider than a belt. Her long, long legs were bare to mid-thigh, below which she wore black woollen stockings which looked like overlong socks. On her feet she wore impractical, leopard-skin ankle boots with the highest, spikiest heels Susie had ever seen outside the pages of a fashion magazine.

With her coffee-coloured skin, her long, frizzy black hair, her big, slanted eyes outlined heavily with black kohl and her full lips painted a shiny, vinyl-red, Holly was every inch Susie's idea of a model. She instantly felt reassured by the other girl's friendly smile and her initial wariness began to recede.

'Let's go then, shall we?' Holly said, picking up a shoulder bag from the floor.

Glancing at Sebastian, Susie saw he was preoccupied with his cameras.

'Will I see you later?' she asked him.

He turned and treated her to one of the heart-stopping grins that had attracted her to him from the start.

'Sure, babe – we'll go out to dinner in a few days, right?'

'A few days?' Susie was bewildered. Surely she would see him daily?

'You're going to be a very busy girl this week. Holly will look after you. Just do as she says and everything will be fine.'

He turned away, leaving Susie staring at his back. What did he mean?

'Coming?' Holly asked from the doorway.

Still bewildered, Susie followed her out of the door, lugging her heavy case behind her.

The next day passed in a whirl for Susie. First Holly took her to have her legs, underarms and bikini-line waxed before allowing her the comfort of a facial, followed by a make-up lesson. Next came the hairdresser, who highlighted her long blond hair before cutting it into a sharp, chin-length bob.

By the time she had been manicured and pedicured, pummelled and smoothed, Susie felt exhausted.

'How do you go through with all this on a regular basis?' she asked, admiring Holly's smooth, blemish-free skin and immaculate presentation.

Holly shrugged. 'It's all part of the job. This is my product, isn't it?' she said, pointing at her lovely face with one long, red-tipped finger. 'So's yours, or at least, it will be. You wouldn't want to try to flog an inferior product, would you?'

Holly had a way of putting things that made Susie smile. She was so matter of fact about everything, it gave the younger girl confidence when her own supply was flagging.

They were sitting in Holly's small flat where Susie was staying, sleeping on the sofa bed in the living room. Holly told her that once she started 'paying her way' as she put it, Sebastian would no doubt find something similar for her.

Meanwhile, Susie was quite happy to camp out in Holly's living room, glad of the company. Alone, she suspected, she would brood on the row she had had with Diana, and on Adam's kiss. Both things that would undermine her newfound independence. Both dangerous.

In the evening they went to a wine bar in Soho, Susie dressed in the most sophisticated outfit she owned: the little black dress she had worn when Sebastian came to dinner at the farmhouse. There, it had seemed like the height of chic. Here, amongst the metropolis's smartest, she felt like a gauche, naïve hick from the sticks. Convinced that everyone was eyeing her and finding her wanting, Susie tried to melt into the background with her glass of wine.

Holly, however, was having none of it. 'Come and meet Meg and Patsy,' she said, dragging her by the hand to the bar. 'Don't hide yourself away!' she hissed in Susie's ear. 'You've got to do it for yourself in this town. Don't rely on Seb to do it for you.'

Wondering what on earth she meant, Susie smiled and posed and drank, until she realised with a small start of surprise that she was actually beginning to enjoy herself.

Wasn't this what she had come to London for? she asked herself as she looked around the bar at all the trendy people, all laughing and smiling and having fun. And she was one of them! Already. Accepted without question.

The next few days passed in much the same fashion: an exhausting round of shopping and beauty treatments during the day and endless parties at night. And Holly was always by her side, like a guardian angel, directing her, watching over her approvingly, as if she were undergoing some sort of ritual test.

It wasn't until the weekend that Susie saw Sebastian again.

'Hey, babe – let's look at you!'

He took both her hands in his and held her at arms' length so that he could look her up and down. Susie knew she was holding her breath, needing his approval even though she knew she looked good.

She was wearing the slim-fitting white tube dress that Holly had helped her choose the day before. It was simple in style: scoop necked and sleeveless, the skirt ending a good six inches above her knees. Her smooth, expertly depilated legs had, like the rest of her body, been subjected to an expensive tanning treatment, which gave them a healthy glow.

She had been practising the techniques learned in her make-up lesson and knew that her grooming was immaculate. As was her hair, freshly blow-dried that morning, and her acrylic nails, which she was still getting used to. All in all, Holly had helped her to create quite a package.

'What a transformation!'

Susie basked in the warmth of Sebastian's approval, aware that she had been nervous of his reaction.

'How's she been getting on, Holly?'

'She's a natural, aren't you, Susie?'

'The name will have to change ... what do you think? Suzanne? Susanna?'

'How about Suki?'

'Yeah – I like it!'

Susie listened as the two discussed her as if she weren't there.

'I like my name,' she ventured timidly.

Sebastian waved impatiently at her.

'Of course you do, sweetheart, but Suki has more impact, more *chutzpah*. Trust me on this – Susie might be cute, but Suki will be a star!'

Susie glanced at Holly, who nodded encouragingly.

'All right,' she agreed eventually. 'If you think it'll help.'

'Good girl,' Sebastian said, kissing her lightly on the forehead. 'We'll start taking some photographs on Monday. Meanwhile, it's time to crack open the champagne. Hadn't you got a date for tonight, Holly?'

Holly looked as if she might be about to disagree but as Sebastian raised an eyebrow, she nodded.

'That's right – I almost forgot!' she said with a brightness that seemed forced.

'Shame,' Sebastian said with a smile that oozed charm, 'I'd planned to take both you girls out to celebrate – now it'll just have to be me and Suki.'

Susie felt her throat contract as the heat of his gaze came to rest on her.

'I . . . er . . . celebrate what?' she asked through lips which suddenly felt dry.

Sebastian's eyes ran over her once more, the unmistakably proprietorial glint in them causing her to shiver.

'The making of Suki,' he said.

He did not take her to any of the bars or clubs she had become used to frequenting with Holly. Instead their taxi drove slowly through the busy West End streets, pulling up outside a glass-fronted restaurant whose name even Susie recognised.

She tried to hide the fact that she was impressed, but knew her cheeks were flushed and her eyes wide as they walked in and were shown immediately to a corner table. Sebastian seemed to be well known by the staff who fussed discreetly around them until they were comfortably seated at the glass-topped, chrome-legged table which was so small their knees touched beneath it.

As they had walked across the room, Susie was aware that they were attracting attention, but if Sebastian knew any of the people who were looking at them, he gave no indication at all, he seemed to have eyes only for Susie. Being the focus of his attention was intoxicating: it made her feel cared for and very, very special.

She felt pretty tonight in a floaty, cornflower-blue dress which barely skimmed her knees, her bare feet encased in the softest leather sandals. Their high heels made her walk with a roll to her hips which made her feel intensely feminine, almost fragile.

Sebastian was wearing an off-white jacket over a pale lavender shirt, open at the neck. His trousers were washing-powder-commercial white, cinched in at his slender waist by a soft leather belt in a brave shade of violet. Susie thought he looked wonderful.

'What would you like to eat?' he asked her as they were handed the menu.

Susie glanced at the list of elaborately described dishes, but could not concentrate.

'You order for me,' she said, listening to the cadences of his voice as he ordered them both grilled trout and salad.

'You're looking very lovely tonight,' he said, as the waiter walked away.

'Thank you. I was just thinking the same thing about you!'

Sebastian laughed and Susie blushed, realising she had sounded gauche. He caught her hand across the table.

'You are the most charming girl, Susie – so ... unspoiled. I can't wait to capture that quality about you on camera.'

It didn't matter what he was saying. Susie noticed that he had used her real name and not her new, professional one, and was glad, but his gaze, coupled with the way he was circling her palm with the pad of his thumb, was doing strange things to her equilibrium, making it difficult to think straight.

She struggled to keep up the new, sophisticated veneer which Holly had taught her, but a part of her was still very much back in Wales, barely out of school.

'You seem nervous,' Sebastian said as she toyed with her meal.

'No! No, I'm not!' she answered, alarmed that he had seen through her so easily.

He laughed softly. 'It's all right,' he told her in an undertone. 'I'm going to look after you. Everything will be just fine.'

Their eyes met across the table and Susie knew

exactly what he meant. There would be no chaste kiss or stolen caresses at the door of the flat tonight. Sebastian intended to take their relationship a step further.

Briefly, very briefly, Susie wondered whether she should call a halt now. Was this really the man with whom she wanted to share her first time? His leg pressed insistently against hers under the table and she felt a familiar little shiver race along her thigh. It would be all right, she told herself firmly, she was ready.

'I know,' she whispered.

Once the decision was made, the rest of the meal passed in a blur. Susie was sure the food was delicious, the wine first class, the service attentive, but she neither tasted nor saw anything. Sebastian filled her vision and all her attention remained focused purely on him, all evening.

The way he touched his fingertips against hers as they rested on the table, the insistent press of his knees against hers beneath the table, the sensuous movement of his cool, firm lips as they shaped words she barely heard: all these things served to heighten her awareness, making the anticipation almost unbearable.

She was aware that her breasts had become ultra-sensitive, the bra-less tips rubbing against the soft leaves of fabric as she leaned forward to catch what he was saying. Her sex had grown moist, the inner folds of sensitive flesh swelling so that they moved against each other as she sat back in her seat, creating a friction which stimulated her still further, making it difficult to breathe.

When she looked into Sebastian's eyes, she saw her own desire reflected in the dark pools of his pupils and she knew that her need was written clearly across her face. Somehow, though, she did not mind that he knew, she wanted him to see the strength of her feelings so that he would realise how much she wanted him.

When their dessert plates had been removed, he put a protective arm around her shoulder and steered her out of the restaurant into a waiting cab. Susie couldn't contain a stab of disappointment when he gave the address of Holly's flat.

'But—'

'Holly won't be back tonight,' he said, silencing her with a forefinger placed gently against her lips. Then his mouth replaced his finger and he was kissing her, his lips hungry, his tongue probing, demanding, and Susie's head began to swim. *This* was what she had been waiting for, it was what she had wanted all evening. No wonder she hadn't been able to do justice to her meal – her hunger had had nothing to do with food and everything to do with the urgent thrust of Sebastian's tongue in her mouth.

The journey back to the flat seemed to take no time at all. In the lift on the way up, Susie allowed herself to be carried along by the strength of Sebastian's passion, closing her mind once and for all to caution. She had always held herself aloof with the boys at home, waiting for the right man to teach her what lovemaking was all about. From the moment she set eyes on Sebastian Semple, she had known that he could be that man. Now all she had to do was go with the flow and not allow her virginal misgivings to ruin everything.

As Sebastian had predicted, the flat was empty when they arrived. Susie began to protest when he steered her into Holly's bedroom, but he swallowed her words with a kiss, his hands already unzipping her dress.

Susie felt a cold chill of panic shoot through her

stomach. As if realising he was moving too fast, Sebastian brought his hands up to cup her face. His kisses became softer, more tender, and Susie relaxed again.

This was how she had imagined it would be – a man's hands soft against her skin, whispered words of adulation warm against her hair . . .

Tendrils of excitement curled through her body like wisps of smoke on the evening air. Her limbs felt heavy, her stomach tense with anticipation as Sebastian edged her towards the bed. She felt it behind her knees and clung to him, afraid that she would fall.

His lips hardened against hers and his caresses became firmer, more demanding. Susie gasped against his mouth as he fondled her breasts almost roughly, feeling them swell in response, the nipples puckering into two aching little peaks of need.

Breaking away from her lips, he dipped his head so that he could suck first one, then the other burgeoning little promontory into his mouth, through the fabric of her dress. His mouth was hot, his teeth scraping the tender flesh of her areolae, yet despite his roughness, or perhaps because of it, Susie found that she was panting, wanting release more than she had ever wanted it before.

'*Please* . . .' she gasped, not sure what it was she was pleading for, only knowing that she wanted it to go on.

She collapsed on to the bed without protest, revelling in the weight of Sebastian's hard, male body pressing her into the mattress. He prised her thighs apart with one knee, while with one hand he sought to push her dress up, over her waist.

Susie felt a moment's self-consciousness as he exposed the tiny white panties which barely covered

139

her sex. Then Sebastian ripped them away with one determined tug, and she was stripped of even that inadequate barrier between them.

She was trembling as he feasted his eyes on her exposed, open sex. From her habit of watching herself in the mirror, she knew exactly what he could see. She knew, too, that she was wet, her tender flesh leaves glistening with the evidence of her arousal. His eyes were half closed, his expression one of wholly masculine satisfaction as he murmured, 'Beautiful, just beautiful. Open wider, baby, I've got something for you.'

Though his wasn't the first penis Susie had ever seen, it was certainly the thickest. Her eyes widened as it sprung like a coiled snake from his trousers, its tip beaded with moisture, glinting at her almost threateningly. Seeing her expression, he grinned.

'Touch it,' he said, grasping her hand and forcing it towards his groin.

With a kind of repelled fascination, Susie grasped the swollen stem, feeling it throb hotly against her palm as she moved it experimentally along the shaft.

'Oh, yesss . . .' he hissed, closing his eyes for a second and swallowing hard.

When he opened them again, his pupils had expanded so that they almost covered the iris, and his gaze was hot and unfocused. Slipping his fingers between her legs, he pressed her clitoris against her pubic bone and rolled it, making her cry out with the intensity of the sensation that shot through her.

Kneeling between her thighs, Sebastian unrolled a condom over his tumescent shaft, then rubbed its head against the sensitive flesh of her labia. Susie gritted her teeth as he sank slowly inside her, wincing at the sharp stab of pain as he burrowed deeper, twisting his hips so that he could knock against the neck of her womb.

'Oh, God. . . !' she whispered, her voice cracking with emotion as the walls of her vagina pulsated around him. She had never imagined it would be so intense.

For a few seconds he held himself there, allowing her to grow used to the sensation of fullness before starting to move. Susie clung to his shoulders as he began to saw back and forth. His skin was hot and slippery, the friction as he slid against her flesh creating a heat which threatened to overwhelm her.

Susie closed her eyes, blocking out everything but the sense of possession, clenching her inner muscles around the stem of his marauding cock, making the sensations ripple inside her.

Opening her eyes again, Susie saw that Sebastian seemed to be oblivious to her presence as he heaved and grunted his way towards climax. His face was set in an expression of extreme concentration, his eyes fixed on a point on the wall just above her head. He was breathing heavily, his lips parted moistly, a film of sweat beading his forehead.

Susie felt odd, as if she were somehow outside of herself, looking down on the two of them rolling together on Holly's bed, consumed by, yet curiously detached from the scene. Whilst on the one hand she was completely caught up by what was happening, on the other she realised she was watching, coolly assessing, the events which were unfolding and analysing her own reactions.

She was aware that something had softened deep in her womb, a kind of slow, uncurling sensation which made it contract, almost painfully. Suddenly, her muscles pulsed, sending a fresh wave of feeling through her which, in turn, transmitted itself to Sebastian. The tendons in his neck stood out like cords as he strained to reach his climax.

Susie's nails dug into his shoulders as she crested the peak, seconds before he let out his breath on a pent-up gasp, collapsing across her like a deflated balloon.

Her own orgasm dwindled away, leaving her feeling strangely unsatisfied as Sebastian rolled off her and on to his back. Flinging one arm across his forehead, he closed his eyes, letting out a long, low whistle between his teeth.

'Not bad, baby,' he said, when he had enough breath to speak, 'not bad at all for the first time.'

Susie said nothing, but lay very still beside him as he fell asleep. Her feelings were in turmoil, her body aching for more than this brief glimpse of bliss. Slowly, she allowed her hand to slip between her legs. Her sex flesh was still swollen and wet with their combined juices, but it also felt sore and bruised. Wincing slightly, she found her clitoris and stroked it softly, her caress gently stimulating.

A familiar, warm glow spread through her as she worked her way quietly to climax, the moment of release sweet and gentle, comforting her, leaving her physically satisfied. Yet still sleep eluded her, and as she lay naked in the darkness on top of Holly's bed, listening to Sebastian's contented snores, she promised herself that she would find out more about sex. There had to be more between two people than what she had just experienced with Sebastian and, though she was physically replete, she felt strangely empty inside, as if the experience had failed to touch her in a way that was so fundamental, it virtually nullified the physical act.

Turning her head, she watched Sebastian as he slept,

blissfully ignorant of her restlessness. He'd had his chance, she thought coldly. From now on she would look for satisfaction elsewhere.

Chapter Nine

RHIORDAN AND ADAM walked together across the lower field of the Jones Farm. In the month since Susie had left, they had seen far less of each other, and Rhiordan had the distinct feeling that Adam had been, if not exactly avoiding her, then certainly cooler towards their relationship.

To her frustration, there hadn't been a repeat of the night he had spent with her and her mother. Megan was philosophical about it, but Rhiordan had hoped it might become a regular occurrence, as it had with previous boyfriends.

At first she had worried that the game had put him off in some way, but he had made love to her happily enough three times since. The problem was, for her three times in a month was nowhere near enough, especially since the last time had been rather less than satisfactory. She still fancied him like crazy and his apparent preoccupation was driving her mad.

Today he was, if anything, even more quiet and preoccupied than normal, so when the heavens opened, soaking them to the skin, Rhiordan grabbed his hand and ran with him to the barn in the lower part of the field, seeing the shower as a blessing in disguise.

'Come on!' she shouted as the downpour grew heavier, 'we'll drown in this lot!'

They were laughing as they reached the barn. Inside, the air was still and musty but warm, and they lost no time in stripping off their wet clothes. Adam caught the hungry glint in Rhiordan's eyes and felt his heart rate quicken. If only he could hang on to that feeling . . .

Her naked flesh was warm and pliant as he took her into his arms and kissed her. He felt the hardening of her nipples against the wall of his chest and the soft press of her belly against his, and his body responded independently of his mind, his cock rising between them, potent and willing as ever.

Rhiordan made a small, contented sound in the back of her throat and squirmed provocatively against him.

'Mmm – that feels good, lover,' she murmured. Her lips and tongue felt hot as they explored his mouth, running over his chin and down his throat like a cat's.

Adam leaned back against the supporting beam and closed his eyes. Rhiordan's skin felt like damp silk as she slid to her knees in front of him, her hands and lips seeking the tumescent shaft of his penis. He felt the familiar thrill of sensation start in the pit of his belly as she enclosed him in her fist and moved the outer flesh back and forth across his rigid length.

He felt hot, yet shivery where he had been caught in the rain, almost as if he was running a fever. He could hear the angry spatter of the rain against the ancient tiled roof of the barn and the smell of musty hay filled his nostrils. As Rhiordan's lips enfolded the tip of his penis, he shuddered, bracing his feet on the cold stone floor to steady himself.

Almost at once, his desire seemed to subside, slipping away in direct proportion to the amount of stimulation she was giving him. Adam tried to concentrate, but it was no use; he couldn't seem to keep his mind on the moment.

On her knees in front of him, Rhiordan was fellating him enthusiastically, with every appearance of enjoyment. It was some moments before she realised something was wrong.

'Do you want to talk about it?' she asked when they had both dressed.

Adam shrugged, looking away to hide his embarrassment. 'I'm sorry,' he said. 'It's not something that's ever happened to me before.'

They left the barn and walked together across the field that led to the road.

'You've been like this ever since Susie left,' Rhiordan said after a few minutes.

'I don't think—'

'I do. And I think it's about time you stopped kidding yourself. Have you heard from her at all?'

Adam shook his head. There hadn't been a word from Susie since the day she left. Diana was frantic with worry, and he had to restrain himself daily from jumping on a train and going after her, to wring her selfish, inconsiderate little neck.

'This came yesterday.'

He took the postcard she handed him and turned it over. '*Hi!*' it read, '*London is everything I dreamed of, and more! Sebastian has me working hard, but still there's plenty of time for partying. Write to me soon. xxx*' Underneath she had printed an address.

'Do you mind if I keep this?' he asked, trying to ignore the pang it caused him to know that Susie had written to Rhiordan rather than to him ... or her mother.

146

Rhiordan shrugged. 'Go ahead.'

'I'll show it to Diana – ease her mind a little. Do you want to go for a drink later?'

The invitation was half-hearted and they both knew it. Rhiordan stopped walking and made him face her.

'Look, Adam, whatever it was we had together has obviously fizzled out, so why don't we call it a day while we're still friends?'

Taken aback, Adam began to protest, but she silenced him by placing her forefinger softly against his lips.

'Ssh!' she said. Her smile was sad, but far from heart-broken. 'We've always been honest with each other, haven't we?'

Adam nodded.

'Well, let me be honest now. I have ... *needs*, you know? I get edgy if I don't get those needs satisfied every day. In a small village like this, everyone knows everyone else's business, so it's not possible to run more than one man at a time, at least, not discreetly. You'd hear, sooner than later.'

'You've got someone else?' Adam was ashamed that he felt only relief at the news.

'Let's just say I've got someone in mind. Lets you off the hook, doesn't it?' she added mischievously.

Adam laughed and hugged her. 'I wish you nothing but happiness,' he said, meaning every word.

'It's been fun, hasn't it?' she said, leaning back to scan his face.

'It sure has. You're a fine girl, Rhiordan Davis.'

'I know. And so's Susie, when you get to know her. But then, you know that, don't you, Adam?'

'I don't know what you mean.'

She laughed softly. 'Yes you do. So give us a kiss and I'll be on my way.'

He obliged, acknowledging a fleeting regret that he wouldn't be seeing so much of her in the future. Her good-humoured, undemanding company had been a godsend when he had first arrived in the country, and he would always be glad of her friendship. But she was right; something intangible, but important, seemed to have gone missing, and there was no point in carrying on their relationship without it.

'See you around,' she said as she left him.

He watched her stride across the field, admiring the way her bottom moved beneath the thin cotton of her dress as she walked. As she reached the gate, she turned to give him a wave.

'Give me a call if you fancy a fuck for old time's sake!' she called, flashing him a cheeky grin as she walked away.

Adam laughed and let her go without regret or self-reproach. Then he remembered Susie's postcard and his heart felt leaden. Why couldn't he let her go so easily?

Maybe if they'd done more than kiss . . . ? That was probably the problem – suppressed lust just wasn't his style. Maybe he should go to London, seek her out and make her confront what was between them. Once desire had been slaked and their relationship was allowed to run its course, maybe then he'd be able to stop thinking about her night and day.

That thought cheered him a little. Perhaps one day he'd act on his instincts. Meanwhile, he needed to go back to the house and let Diana know that her daughter was apparently okay.

As Susie made her way back to Holly's flat, her feet dragged. The shoes she was wearing were too small and after a whole morning of lugging her portfolio around uninterested fashion editors' offices, they were pinching like hell. All she wanted was a hot bath, followed by a cup of sweet tea with her feet up on the sofa.

Opening the door to the flat, she knew immediately that Holly was not alone. For a start, the bedroom door was wide open and she could see her friend's long, dark limbs entangled intimately with Sebastian's golden body as they heaved and grunted together towards climax.

Susie dropped her portfolio on to the carpet and sank down on the sofa.

'Hi, Holly, I'm back,' she called. Slipping off her shoes, she massaged her aching feet. The first time she had seen Sebastian and Holly screwing she had been mortified. If someone had told her then that she would be this blasé about the whole thing within five short weeks, she would never have believed them.

The noise in the bedroom was reaching a crescendo. Susie lay back on the sofa and closed her eyes. She wished she could close her ears too, but there was no chance of getting away from the noise in the small flat.

Though she had become used to it, the sound of Holly and Sebastian having sex still embarrassed her. There was something about their flamboyant exhibitionism that made her feel uneasy. It was almost as if she were a captive audience, forced into the role of voyeur.

The first time it happened, she had been sleeping on the bed-settee after they had all been out for a drink to celebrate her 'transformation', when she was woken in the middle of the night by a muffled groan. As she lay in the unfamiliar darkness, she heard Holly giggle softly, then Sebastian's smooth, unmistakable voice whispering, 'Keep it quiet, baby – I don't want to frighten off the new chick in the nest.'

For a few minutes, Susie had lain rigid beneath the duvet, wondering whether to pretend to continue sleeping, or whether to make a great show of waking up so that they would stop. After a few minutes, though, she realised that they were so wrapped up in each other that it was obvious that they probably wouldn't notice if she got up and went into the bedroom to watch.

But the sound of them making love was disturbing, and it made her feel hot and restless. That first night she had sat up slowly and looked over the back of the bed-settee. From there, she could see right into Holly's room and the sight that met her eyes made her mouth run dry. Both naked, Holly and Sebastian rolled on the satin sheets, their arms and legs entangling as they moved together in a choreographed dance of desire.

She had lain back on the sofa, holding herself very, very still, absurdly embarrassed that she could hear them. The soft sighs and guttural moans had made her feel hot all over; her skin prickled and her breasts ached.

If she closed her eyes, she could remember the feel of Adam's hard, strong body pressing against the softness of hers, could recall the delicious yielding of her own flesh against his. Was that what Holly felt like as Sebastian moved inside her? And, if so, why hadn't she felt the same?

Forgetting to keep him out of her mind, in her imagination she surrendered completely to Adam. She pictured the concentration on his face as he possessed her, fantasised about the feel of his cock as he slipped it slowly, inch by inch into the hot, welcoming passage of her pussy . . .

Suddenly, she missed home so badly it was like a

physical ache deep in her belly. All the feelings she had suppressed during the mad whirl of the previous week hit her with the force of a sledgehammer, leaving her winded. She missed her home, her friends and her mother; everything that was familiar, everything she had wanted to escape for so long.

But most of all, she wanted Adam lying alongside her on the sofa, Adam's hands and lips roaming her body as Sebastian's had, Adam's arms around her, keeping her safe. Adam's hard, strong body inside her, becoming part of her with each thrust, making her his . . .

That was then – the first time she had seen Sebastian and Holly making love. Now Susie prided herself on what she believed to be her sophisticated acceptance of the casual sex taking place mere feet away from her. She knew the participants well enough now to know that it *was* casual, and she no longer felt the need to make up false yearnings for a man she had kissed only once, and even then as an aberration.

To prove to herself that she had settled in to her new, cosmopolitan life, she had sent a postcard to Rhiordan, knowing that she would probably show it to Adam and that he would read the message between the lines: *See how well I'm doing without you – I don't need you at all!*

That would show him, make him start to realise that her dreams of becoming a model weren't the absurd fantasies of a silly adolescent girl, but the realistic plans of a strong woman. For she had grown up a lot since she arrived in London. He wouldn't recognise her as the frustrated young girl who had stood up to her mother.

Thinking of Diana gave her a pang. Soon she would feel confident enough to be able to send her a letter, maybe even ring her. Meanwhile, Rhiordan would tell her that she was all right and Diana didn't need to worry.

'How did you get on?'

Susie jumped as Sebastian meandered into the living room, wearing nothing but a minuscule white towel around his waist.

'Oh . . . er . . . not so good,' she admitted, trying not to look at his shower-wet hair, or his exposed, hair-roughened naked skin.

The sight of him aroused her and he knew this for he seemed to make a point of wandering around the flat in next to nothing.

Now he lit up a cigarette and regarded her thoughtfully through a cloud of smoke. 'It's time you started to pay your way,' he said evenly after a few minutes.

'What . . . what do you mean?' Susie asked him, frowning uneasily.

'All this—' he waved his cigarette in a circle '—your hair, your clothes, your bed and board. It doesn't come free, you know. Who do you think pays for it all?'

'You do, Sebastian,' Susie answered meekly, feeling far from the strong, confident woman she had imagined herself to be only minutes before.

'That's right. And it's not out of the goodness of my heart; all this serves a purpose. It's about time I saw a return from my investment, wouldn't you say?'

Holly came into the living room, fastening her cotton robe around her waist as she did so.

'Oh, give her a bit more time, Seb, she—'

'Shut up.'

Seemingly oblivious to the shocked silence, he picked up Susie's portfolio and flicked absently through the photographs.

'Maybe you haven't got what it takes,' he mused, half to himself.

Susie suppressed a cold shiver. 'Oh, but, the editor of *Teen* said—'

'*Teen?*' Sebastian sneered. 'You don't want to listen to anything they say. Amateurs. No, I have something you might be suited to. Holly, make sure she gets into the studio by midday tomorrow. It's time *Suki* here got to work.'

The two girls looked at each other as he strode back into the bedroom. Susie guessed that Holly's smile was meant to be reassuring, but it seemed sickly and didn't quite reach her eyes.

'Come on,' she said, as if trying to cheer up a fearful child. 'Let's get our glad rags on and hit the town.'

'But . . . if I'm working tomorrow . . . ?'

'He doesn't want you there until midday. There's a male act on at the *Four Feathers*. Baby oil and leather jock straps – Mm-mmm!'

Susie laughed, grateful to Holly for lightening the mood. Holly grinned, apparently feeling the same way.

'We'll wait until he leaves, then we'll party.'

The *Four Feathers* was a pub not far from the flat, which Holly called her 'time off' place. Susie guessed that she meant it was somewhere she could really relax and not feel as if she was marketing her 'product' all the time. Susie had been there only once before, on a Sunday lunchtime.

She hadn't liked it much – it was loud and crowded and smoky, and nobody gave a stuff who they were, or what they were trying to be. Though she could see that might be attractive to Holly, who had been at the posing game for far longer than she had, Susie enjoyed the attention she got at the trendy bars and clubs they usually went to. The *Four Feathers* felt too ordinary, too much like everything she had come to London to get away from.

As they walked in that evening, Susie could sense that the atmosphere was different. For a start, the clientele consisted mainly of women, though there were several men propping up the bar, trying to look macho and uninterested in what was going on around them. Holly paid a visit to the ladies', then headed for the bar.

'We're just in time!' she hissed in Susie's ear after she'd bought them two bottles of beer each. 'C'mon, I want a front row view.'

She elbowed her way through the press of women, dragging Susie along behind her, totally oblivious to the complaints and insults from those she pushed aside.

'Here,' she said, pushing Susie up against the raised platform at the front. 'Stand your ground – it'll be worth the bruised ribs in the long run!'

Almost immediately, the music started and three bronzed, well-muscled men in conservative looking three-piece suits strutted on to the stage. Casting amused, haughty glances across the sea of female watchers, who had erupted into a cacophony of yells and whistles as they arrived on stage, they began to dance.

Susie had never seen anything like it. As the men began to strip off their clothes, the crowd went wild, surging forward and nearly crushing her against the makeshift stage. Casting a sidelong glance at Holly, she saw that her friend was whooping along with the best of them, taking long gulps of her beer and leering at the now near-naked dancers.

'Hi, Holly,' one of them shouted as he bent low near them. 'Come to give us a hand again?'

'You bet – whatever you want!' She laughed, leaning forward to kiss him on the mouth.

Susie watched, her own mouth hanging open in amazement at Holly's nerve. The dancer was tall and broad, his velvet-textured black skin gleaming with oil under the spotlights, his long hair plaited and tied back in a pony-tail to expose the sharp, lean lines of his face. He was beautiful, like a sculpture, lovingly crafted, but untouchable. Though not by Holly. Her hands were everywhere: splayed across his chest, running over his shoulders, reaching for the lurid red leather g-string, which was all he wore.

Playfully, to good-natured boos from the audience, he slapped her hand away.

'How about your friend?' he asked.

Holly glanced at Susie.

'You *know* him?' Susie squeaked.

Holly laughed. Her eyes were overbright, her pupils dilated and she seemed edgy and over-excitable. Turning back to the dancer who was gyrating lewdly in front of her, she shook her head.

'She's just a baby,' she said, 'you leave her alone!'

Affronted, Susie glared at her friend, then caught the dancer's eye. The look she surprised there made her suck in her breath. It was both speculative and predatory and horribly, excitingly sexy. Susie watched, mesmerised, as he squirmed along the stage, making it part of the act, then bent over her so that her face was almost level with his groin. She caught the tang of fresh male sweat and a less familiar, more earthy scent which made her throat and mouth run dry.

Barely restrained by his g-string, his cock was

155

bursting to get out. This close, she could see the bulbous purple tip peeking over the top, ready to be released.

He bent low, moving his lips close to her ear.

'See you later,' he murmured.

His breath was hot against her ear and Susie thought she would climax there and then. She felt almost bereft as he danced playfully away from her and joined his colleagues who, she realised now that the hypnotic presence of the man dancing in front of her had been removed, were busy caressing and kissing Holly in the middle of the stage.

How had she got up there? Susie could barely credit that she had not noticed her friend clambering on to the stage, yet there was the evidence before her very eyes. Holly had made herself part of the act, and from the look on her lovely face, she was enjoying every minute.

She was moving with all the skill of a professional dancer, and as two of the men lifted her in their arms, giving the third man free rein to run his large hands all over her body, she stretched like a cat between them and smiled widely at the audience.

The women went berserk, egging her on, calling for them to strip her, for her to strip them . . . Susie felt her face glow with mortification, barely able to believe her own eyes and ears. It was all too much, too over the top . . .

Finally, Holly was deposited back into the audience and the three men spun into a dance routine which culminated in the removal with a flourish of the red leather g-strings.

The crowd went wild, and for a moment Susie thought they were going to rush the platform. She clung to Holly as the other girl took her hand and made her way backstage. The door to the dressing room was barred by a stagehand so wide he almost filled the doorway. To Susie's amazement, he seemed to recognise Holly and, with a big grin, he let her inside.

'Hey, Holly!' the black dancer cried as he saw her. 'Have you come to party?'

'You betcha! But I'll need to call a cab for Susie here first.'

'What? But I don't want to go home!' Susie protested. 'Can't I come to the party too?'

They all laughed, making her frown.

'Hey, if she wants to join us . . .' one of the others said, but Holly was firm.

'No, she's not into it,' Holly said firmly. Turning to Susie, she spoke quietly into her ear. 'Do me a favour, Susie, I want a little R and R here, know what I mean?'

Susie didn't, but she didn't want to admit that to Holly. 'You don't have to worry about me,' she said with far more confidence than she was feeling. But Holly shook her head.

'Be a good girl and go home.'

'I've got a better idea – have a drink, Susie girl, and rest your feet,' the dancer who had whispered in her ear suggested.

Piqued at the way Holly had tried to dismiss her, Susie took the glass she was offered and, feeling thirsty, drank its contents quickly. The three dancers and Holly were talking animatedly amongst themselves, completely ignoring her, so she sat down on a hard, moquette-covered chair and leaned back her head.

After what seemed like only a few moments she found she was incredibly tired. Though she could hear the others talking and laughing, she found she could not quite make out what they were saying any more.

She felt curiously detached, removed from the situation in a way that made her feel strange.

'I think I'll just have a little sleep,' she slurred to no one in particular. She didn't remember anything else.

The next morning, Susie had a hangover like no other hangover she'd ever had before. When Holly came to wake her at eleven she pulled the duvet over her head and squeezed her eyes tight shut against the glare of the sunlight that streamed in when Holly opened the living room blind.

'C'mon, Suki, you've got to get up! I have to get you across town for Sebastian.'

'Go away!' Susie mumbled. Her tongue felt huge in her mouth and the words sounded thick and distorted. She whimpered as Holly shook her roughly by the shoulder.

'Wake up, girl, we've got to get moving!'

A note of urgency in the other girl's voice penetrated the fog in Susie's brain. She tried to open her eyes but the attempt was painful; her eyeballs felt gritty and sore and the lids seemed to weigh too much.

She allowed herself to be pulled to her feet and staggered, still with eyes half closed, into the shower. The cool water made her gasp and she lifted her face to the spray, welcoming the cleansing deluge.

It would have been good to linger, but Holly had other ideas. Switching off the taps, she pulled Susie out of the shower and began rubbing her down briskly with a fresh towel.

'Uh . . . I can do that!' Susie protested, snatching ineffectually at the towel.

'No time,' Holly snapped. 'Sebastian'll go out of his tree if he sees the state you're in!'

Susie frowned. Her head was banging mercilessly and her mouth tasted as though she had been chewing a dirty sock. Now that she was awake, she was aware that she could recall very little of the night before. She remembered the show, and the scene in the dressing room afterwards, but after that . . . nothing. How had she got back to the flat?

'Holly?' she said, allowing herself to be dressed by the other girl, standing passively like a doll.

'What?'

'Where did we go last night?'

'Don't you remember?'

'No. Surely I didn't have that much to drink?'

Holly shrugged. 'It was probably the tab Vincent slipped you. You're not used to it, are you?'

Susie stared, her mind turning somersaults. Had she really taken something. 'I . . . I don't remember . . .'

'Don't worry about it. I've lost whole weeks before now,' Holly said airily.

'But . . . I've never taken anything before . . . I can't believe I did! And who's Vincent?'

Holly shot her a strange look. 'How should I know? You're the one who spent all last night dancing with him. Or can't you remember that either?'

At once, like the replay of a film, it came back to her, frame by lurid frame. She remembered the drink they had given her and how strange it had made her feel . . . but then, after the initial wooziness, she had felt a surge of energy, like a bolt of lightning, passing through her body, filling her with excitement. A curious sensation, not unpleasant, but uncomfortable, crept beneath her skin, as if she was itching from the inside.

Suddenly she was supremely conscious of every square centimetre of her flesh. The way her clothes skimmed the fine hairs of her skin, the friction of the gusset of her panties against her swollen sex, the restriction of the fabric across her breasts – all these things made her feel hot and restless and very, very sexy.

Someone had turned on a CD player and the small, smoky room was filled with the sounds of an old Roberta Flack number. Susie felt strong, unfamiliar arms slip around her waist and turned to find herself looking into the greenest eyes she had ever seen.

'I'm Vincent,' he said, and the low, grainy dark-sugar texture of his voice had sent shivers down her spine.

'Sus . . . Suki,' she replied hoarsely.

She didn't want to talk to him, there was no need to know anything about him at all. All she wanted was to feel the hardness of his well-toned young body pressing against the length of hers, his heat assuaging the restless itch which was threatening to overwhelm her.

From then on, Susie's recollection took on a hazy, dream-like quality, made up as much of impressions and sensations as solid, distinct pictures. She knew she had danced with Vincent for a long time, their bodies moving together and apart, teasing, tantalising, entwining with a sensuousness which left her heart beating faster and her skin flushed and hot.

One of the other dancers was sitting in a chair at the side of the room, watching her, his long, dark hair falling across his face, shrouding his expression. Knowing he was watching her, Susie deliberately angled herself so as to give him the most flattering view of her as she undulated in time to the music, using Vincent almost as a masturbatory tool as she straddled his thigh and rubbed herself against him, like a cat.

Vaguely, she was aware that it was a dangerous game she was playing, but somehow that only added to the

160

thrill, making her exaggerate her movements even more, wanting to provoke him.

Holly was dancing with Mark and one of the others. As Mark held her close against him, the fourth man was caressing her bottom through the fabric of her dress with an intense concentration. Susie remembered her shocked excitement as he had slowly, carefully moved the dress up Holly's long, bare thighs to expose her naked buttocks beneath, no more than the white sliver of fabric of her thong panties visible, bisecting her firm bottom cheeks.

As Susie watched, the second man sank to his knees and, parting the ripe peaches of Holly's rear, began to lick slowly along her bottom cleft. Apparently oblivious, Holly barely reacted, resting her head on Mark's broad shoulder with a faraway, dreamy expression on her face.

Vincent turned Susie softly in his arms so that she was facing the trio in the middle of the room, her back pressed hard up against him. She could feel the urgent press of his cock against her bottom and the delicious tension in his arms as he held her, betraying his arousal.

She was aware of the man who had been watching her coming to stand near them, but she was too transfixed by the scene unfolding before her to do anything but watch it, mesmerised.

As if choreographed, Holly slid slowly down Mark's body so that she was on her knees in front of him. The man behind her sank too, barely breaking the rhythm of his licking, his hands firmly on Holly's hips so that her bottom was tilted upward, towards him.

Mark stripped off quickly, his thick, erect cock springing free from his shorts and bobbing in front of him as he knelt down in front of Holly. With a throaty moan of appreciation, Holly sank on to all fours, allowing the man behind her to lift her bottom up high, his knees nudging her thighs apart.

Leaning on her elbows, Holly took the purplish bulb of Mark's cock between her lips and held it there, her pink tongue darting around the rim of the glans, making him shiver visibly.

Susie felt Vincent's hands reach round to cup her breasts in his hands and she arched against him, so turned on she didn't care whose hands they were, so long as he continued to touch her. Her nipples sprang hard against his fingers and he murmured something she could not quite catch against her hair.

Holly had taken the full length of Mark into her mouth now, her head moving up and down as she struggled to take him to the back of her throat. The man behind her had unleashed his own cock and was busy masturbating himself along the crease of her bottom. His eyes were half-closed in concentration, his limbs rigid with the tension of impending orgasm.

Vincent slipped his hands beneath the edge of her blouse and under the confines of her bra. Susie moaned softly, wanting more. He seemed to know exactly what it was she wanted. Roughly now, he tore open the front of her blouse and pulled it off her shoulders and down her arms. Excited by his haste, Susie felt a fresh rush of moisture bathe the swollen flesh between her thighs as he dispensed with her bra, leaving her naked from the waist up.

'Suck her tits, Shaun,' he grunted at the man standing beside them. 'I want to get between her legs.'

His crudeness served only to intensify Susie's arousal. She gasped as he rucked up her skirt and tore away her panties. There was no gentleness about the

162

way in which he plunged his hand between her legs and unerringly found the throbbing, wet nub of her clitoris, but gentleness was the last thing she wanted at that moment. She wanted the firm press of his fingers into her soft, wet flesh and the cruel pinch between finger and thumb of her pleasure bud.

Though she cried out, she thrust her bottom back at the same time, inviting more, and Vincent did not disappoint her. In contrast, Shaun sucked almost reverently on her breasts, rolling the nipples one by one on his tongue, apparently savouring every caress.

Over his head, Susie could see that the two men were close to climax. She watched, wide-eyed as the man behind Holly tensed and stopped his relentless movement back and forth between her buttocks. Suddenly, a wide arc of creamy, white fluid burst from the tip of his penis and spattered in random, viscous droplets across the smooth black skin of Holly's back and bottom.

Susie came then, great crashing waves of sensation rolling through her, making her lean forward heavily against Shaun for support. She closed her eyes to savour the moment, snapping them open again as she heard Mark cry out, not wanting to miss a minute.

As if triggered by the visual stimulus of the other man's climax, Mark let out a low growl of triumph and pumped his seed into the warm, wet confines of Holly's willing mouth. Susie watched, fascinated, as Holly sat back on her heels, looking like a cat who'd been at the cream. Though she was swallowing furiously, a thin trickle of fluid seeped out of the corner of her mouth and dripped on to her chin.

Suddenly, Susie was overwhelmed by a compulsion to go across to the other girl and lick away the stain of ejaculate from her flawless skin. Shaun and Vincent let her go and she immediately forgot about them, seeing only Holly as she crawled across the floor on her hands and knees.

The other girl watched her, wide brown eyes shining with an expression Susie could not read. She had never, ever felt a desire to kiss another woman before, yet at that moment she knew there was nothing else she could possibly do.

Slowly, tentatively, she reached out and touched her fingertips against Holly's face. The tension lengthened between them, creating a cocoon around them which made the men in the room fade away. All they could see was each other, their entire focus was exclusive, powerful in a way Susie had never before experienced.

Though she did not move away, Holly did not make any move towards Susie, she merely watched and waited. Encouraged by her passivity, Susie leaned forward and gently, delicately, lapped at the drying semen with the tip of her tongue.

It tasted slightly saline, but all Susie cared about was the honeyed sweetness of Holly's skin beneath. She made a small, satisfied noise at the back of her throat, licking upward to the corner of the other girl's mouth.

Holly's lips moved, forming a silent 'yes', her warm breath fanning Susie's face like a caress. Slowly, not wanting to rush things, she traced the parting of her lips with the very tip of her tongue.

She felt the other girl's lips tremble and her own tingled in response. Shifting forward slightly, so that they were sitting thigh to thigh on the cold linoleum floor, Susie slipped her hand around the back of Holly's head, cupping the fine bones at the base of her skull in a tender embrace. Gazing into her eyes, she moved slowly to capture her lips between hers.

She had never dreamed that kissing another woman

could be so arousing, but there was no denying the thrill that passed between them as their tongues met in earnest. Despite her recent climax, Susie felt her belly soften, her sex flesh swelling and moistening as Holly leaned almost imperceptibly towards her and their nipples touched for the first time.

It was as if live wires had touched, a current ran through them at every point of contact: lips, hands, breasts. With a muffled cry, Holly's arms came about Susie and pressed her close. Leaving her mouth, Susie kissed a trail down the side of Holly's neck, licking the tender hollow where her collarbones met and then moving further down.

It was wonderful to feel the firm, springy flesh of Holly's breasts in her hands as she stroked and kneaded them, her fingertips straying teasingly across the nipples until the other girl moaned aloud in protest. Dipping her head, she took first one, then the other tumescent nipple between her lips. Sucking, kissing, nipping, she played with Holly's breasts until she begged her to stop.

'Please . . . oh, please . . . lower, Suki . . . *lower* . . .'

Susie did not need to be told twice. Easing her friend on to her back, she explored the gentle swell of her belly with her lips and tongue, nuzzling at the furred mound of her pubis.

'You smell so good,' she murmured against the other girl's sex.

Gently, she peeled back the outer leaves with her thumbs, revealing the scarlet fruit within. Awed by its intricate beauty, Susie's first caress was tentative.

'Touch me the way you like to be touched,' Holly urged, allowing her thighs to fall softly apart, giving her easy access to her molten flesh.

165

Susie closed her eyes for a moment, imagining that she was in Holly's place. How *would* she like to be touched?

Slowly, she trailed the very tip of her tongue lightly along the crease of her outer labia, down one side and up the other. Holly's soft mewl of pleasure encouraged her, making her more bold. Nibbling gently along the edge of her inner lips, she drew the moisture seeping from her up to bathe the engorged bud of her clitoris.

Gently, she swirled her tongue around it, taking care not to touch it directly, knowing that the indirect stimulation would drive the other girl wild. At the same time, she stroked the velvety skin of her inner thighs, setting up a rhythm that made Holly sigh with pleasure.

Susie knew instinctively when the other girl had had enough of the gentle approach. As she pressed the flat of her tongue against the pulsing bud, Holly arched her back and thrust her hips hard against Susie's mouth. Her clitoris seemed to swell against her tongue as it began to throb and Susie lashed it back and forth, knowing exactly how much pressure to apply to bring Holly the optimum amount of satisfaction.

When the other girl fell back, exhausted, into Mark's waiting arms, Susie sat back on her heels, triumphant. Gradually the rest of the room swam back into focus: the music, the room, the men . . . the *possibilities* . . .

No wonder Holly had given her that strange look. Standing, she went over to her and kissed her soundly, full on the lips.

'Of course I remember,' she said grinning. 'How could I forget that?'

Holly's dark cheeks flushed and she dropped her eyes.

'Yes, well ... we haven't got time to talk now, Sebastian will be waiting.'

'But we will ... *talk* ... later?' Susie said.

Now Holly lifted her head and caught her gaze boldly.

'I should certainly hope so,' she replied.

'Good. We'd better catch that tube then, hadn't we?'

The tower block where Sebastian worked looked no more appealing with familiarity. There were still youths hanging aimlessly around the entrance, though none she recognised. The smell of cats' pee in the stairwell was, if anything, even stronger, catching at the back of her throat, and the lift was still out of order.

Arriving at the door, Susie was out of breath.

'Did he have to choose a flat this high up?' she gasped as Holly rapped on the door.

It opened almost at once to reveal a disgruntled Sebastian outlined in the doorway. 'You're late,' he said, directing the comment at Holly.

She didn't seem to be able to hold his eye. 'Sorry – we had a late night.'

For a moment Susie thought he was going to say something; the look he gave Holly was filled with fury. It slipped away almost at once, though, making her wonder if she had imagined it.

'Save yourself for your work, sweetheart,' he said in a couldn't-care-less tone that fooled nobody, 'otherwise you might find that free is *all* you're doing it for.'

Holly blanched and, to Susie's bewilderment, mumbled an apology before walking away.

'Holly?' Susie called after her, but the girl did not turn back.

'Leave her – we've got work to do here,' Sebastian

said. 'That is, if you still want to be a model?' he added nastily.

'Of course I do!' Susie said, stepping inside at once.

He smiled. 'Just checking that full-time party girl isn't more your line.'

Susie wasn't sure what he meant, so she simply followed him meekly into the dimly lit studio.

'Over there,' he said, pushing her lightly towards the chair in the centre of the room.

He flicked a switch and Susie found herself sitting in a pool of white light. Sebastian rolled up his sleeves and surveyed her through the lens.

'You look uptight – relax.'

Susie felt stiff and uncomfortable. Though he had taken plenty of pictures of her like this for her portfolio, there was something about the edgy energy with which he started moving around her with the camera that made her feel uneasy.

'Show me a smile . . . a pout . . . now turn your head to the left . . . that's right. Toss your hair . . .'

Click, click, click – the camera was relentless. As she began to move and pose and perform for its unforgiving eye, Susie felt some of the tension leave her. This was what she liked doing best, after all. This was what she was good at. And Sebastian had said that these shots were for a real job, her first assignment.

The thought made her smile widen and Sebastian nodded approvingly.

'That's right – give me some energy . . . yes . . . this is good stuff, Suki, baby . . . you're a natural for this . . .'

After a few minutes, he changed the roll of film and stopped for a few drags of a cigarette. Susie felt his eyes on her and turned to look quizzically at him.

'You're doing fine, sweetheart,' he told her, flashing

168

her one of his heart-stopping grins. 'Now, I need a few with your top off.'

For a second Susie thought she had misheard him. 'Pardon?'

'Your top – I need some tit shots.'

Susie felt as if the air had thickened around her, making it difficult to breathe.

'I . . . I'm sorry, but I don't want to do any nude work. You said it wouldn't be necessary . . .'

Sebastian laughed unpleasantly. 'Don't be ridiculous, babe, it goes with the territory. Get your tits out.'

It had only just begun to sink in that he was serious. Susie felt hot tears of humiliation sting the back of her throat.

'I . . . I can't,' she whispered.

The very idea of exposing herself like that for the titillation of Sebastian's camera made her feel sick. Impatience seemed to be coming off him in waves, making her feel even more miserable.

'What's the big deal?'

'I just don't want to.'

'Then you might as well pack up and go home to Wales – you'll not get anywhere in this business with that kind of attitude.'

His implacable tone made her panic.

'But couldn't I just do the fashion and catalogue work?'

'Sweetheart, do you think I've paid out over a thousand pounds to groom you just so that you can advertise overcoats? For God's sake, Susie, how naïve are you?' He ran his fingers through his hair, exasperated. Then his tone softened and became wheedling. 'You do still want to be a model, sweetheart, don't you?'

'Yes,' she whispered, dropping her eyes.

'You haven't changed your mind? Because if you have, now is the time to tell me. You can walk away and go home to the valleys right now if you want to. Nobody's stopping you.'

'No! No, I don't want to go,' she told him urgently.

'Then do as I say and you'll make it. You've got a good body, so *use* it. Trust me, its not going to be mucky or tatty. I'm an artist. I'll make you look like a goddess. Come on now,' he said, his voice dropping to a low, hypnotic sing-song. 'Don't cry. Unbutton your top.'

Susie slipped the first button through its buttonhole, exposing the gentle swell of her breasts. Hot tears fell on to her shaking fingers and she didn't seem to be able to stop them. She jumped as the camera flashed.

'Don't stop, baby, this is good. The tears are a nice touch . . . look up at me . . . aah, yes, beautiful . . .'

Sebastian kept up the low-voiced encouragement as Susie finished unbuttoning her top. She shivered as the cool air touched her exposed skin.

'Keep going. Push the top off your shoulders . . . that's right. Good girl, you're doing fine.'

Sebastian's eyes were bright as he watched her and Susie felt a mixture of excitement and distaste. She didn't want to do this, but if she didn't, she knew she would never become a model. She would have to ask Diana and Jack to pay Sebastian back and she would have to go home. After all, there was nothing shameful about bare breasts any more; she was being silly and prudish.

'Put your hands on your hips . . . lean forward, push out your tits . . . smile . . . Lovely!'

Sebastian wasn't angry and exasperated with her any more, he was smiling as he worked his way through roll after roll of film, all the while keeping up a continuous stream of encouragement and flattery.

'I knew you had it in you, sweetheart You're a natural. Didn't I say I would make you a star? Part your lips – that's right. Now put the tip of your finger in your mouth and look straight into the camera . . . Beautiful! You're on your way, baby, trust me.'

Susie tried to smile, but her face felt frozen. She wanted to believe him, but the question she dared not voice would not stop nagging at her. She might be 'on her way' as Sebastian said – but on her way to what?

Chapter Ten

ADAM WASN'T GENERALLY in the habit of browsing along the top shelf of the local supermarket, but since he'd suddenly become an unwilling celibate in the weeks following his split with Rhiordan, he often, to his chagrin, found his eyes straying upward.

He had fantasised once or twice that Diana or Megan might come up behind him and embarrass him, but he had never in his wildest imaginings thought he might see Susie smiling down at him from behind the shrink-wrap.

After double-checking that it was indeed her on the cover, Adam pulled down every copy of the magazine and bought them all. Ignoring the curious, sidelong glances he received from the check-out operators, he drove to every supermarket and newsagent within a ten-mile radius of the farm and bought up all the copies, hoping that no one had recognised the local girl sprawled naked across the cover.

Once home, he took one copy straight to his room and ripped off the shrink-wrap. The spread that starred Susie – or *Suki*, as she was billed – confirmed all his worst fears. No wonder they hadn't heard from her – this work was hardly something she could boast of to her family! If Diana saw this, it would break her heart.

He resolved to go out the next day and clear the shelves throughout Pembrokeshire. Meanwhile his initial dismay turned to fury. This was that sleaze, Sebastian Semple's doing. Susie would never have posed like this willingly.

For a moment, Adam allowed his eyes to dwell on the creamy flawlessness of her naked skin, admiring the shape of her breasts and the soft swell of her belly, below which . . .

'Hell!' He swore aloud as he caught himself hardening at the sight of her coyly covered sex.

How could she? Despite the fact that he knew he had no right, he felt betrayed by her appearance in the magazine. The thought of thousands of men all over the country leering at her, masturbating over her paper image made his blood boil.

It was no good, he couldn't keep leaving things as they were, waiting for Susie to see sense and come home. There was nothing else for it. He would have to go to London himself and track her down.

He waited until the next morning before telling his father what he planned to do. They were busy in the lower barn, but Jack stopped what he was doing and looked at him in amazement when he announced his plans.

'You can't leave now, Adam, we're too busy,' he protested.

'You'll have to get more help from the village. I'm sorry, Dad, but I have to go.'

'Would you mind telling me why?'

Adam sighed, his eyes sliding away from his father's as he looked out over the lush, green Pembrokeshire countryside. He didn't want to have to tell him about

Susie, but he knew he couldn't simply walk out during a busy season without giving some kind of explanation.

'I want to find Susie,' he said at last.

'Susie? Why? What's going on?'

'I think she might be in trouble.'

Jack placed his hand on his son's arm urgently.

'Have you heard something from her? You must tell me, Adam – Diana is going crazy worrying about her.'

'I know, but I don't want Diana to find out about this.' Briefly, he told Jack about the photographs.

Jack swore softly under his breath.

'What was she thinking of, getting herself involved with something like that? You're right – Diana doesn't need to know all the details. But I *will* tell her that you've gone to London to track her down. She'll be glad of that. Thanks, son.' He clapped Adam on the shoulder.

Adam smiled weakly, feeling guilty that Jack obviously thought he was doing this for Diana's sake. He didn't feel ready yet, though, to confide in Jack about his feelings for Susie. Even he didn't fully understand those. They were too new, too confusing to be aired . . .

Susie sat in the cold dressing room and waited to be called for her part in the photo shoot. It was a decent job, modelling underwear for a new line of lingerie, but she couldn't get excited about it. She couldn't seem to get excited about anything much these days.

Holly was working with her on this assignment, but neither girl spoke as they waited. Susie shook her head as the other girl offered her a cigarette, knowing that Holly still hadn't properly come down from the night before. Susie understood now, and she didn't blame her. Pills kept Holly going: they got her up in the morning, then kept her going through the day. In the evening they

174

kept her awake and able to keep up the frantic pace she set herself. Then she took something to make her sleep. It was a vicious cycle that she was neither able, nor willing to break.

'Suki?' The photographer's assistant called her and she walked listlessly on to the set. She could do the job in her sleep, it was so predictable. *Move . . . pout . . . smile . . . give us a flash of your tits . . .* How could it have ended up like this?

She pushed the brief flash of bitterness away, reminding herself that she was merely starting out on the lower rungs of the modelling ladder. As Sebastian said, she had to cut her teeth somewhere; it wouldn't always be like this. No one started out at the top of the profession.

She hadn't expected the work to make her feel so bad about herself, though. This came nowhere near her expectations.

As they wrapped up for the day, Susie briefly considered giving up and going home. But deep down she knew she couldn't do that, not now that her naked body had been splashed in glorious Technicolor across the newsstands. The very thought of what she had let Sebastian persuade her to do made her go cold. Supposing all her friends had seen it? Diana . . . ? *Oh, God, it didn't bear thinking about!*

It made her feel so angry when she thought of the way she had let Sebastian use her . . . yet, in her own defence, she knew she had still been reeling from the events of the night before. If she had been fully in charge of herself . . .

'Suki? It is Suki, isn't it?'

She turned to find a man approaching, looking pleased to see her. He looked vaguely familiar with his long, dark hair and angular face and he obviously thought he knew her. Susie, however, was in no mood for being sociable.

'I'm sorry?' she said, injecting what she hoped would be just enough ice in her tone to warn him off without resorting to being downright rude.

'You don't remember me,' he stated flatly.

He looked so crestfallen that Susie could not help but melt a little.

'Your face is familiar, but I'm afraid I can't quite place your name . . . ?'

'That's okay,' he said, brightening visibly. 'We weren't exactly introduced. It's Shaun . . . remember? From the strip club?'

As she took his proffered hand, Susie remembered.

'Of course – I'm sorry, I wasn't too clear-headed that night.'

He laughed, a pleasant, uncomplicated sound. 'None of us were, but . . . wow!'

Susie laughed with him. 'Quite. What are you doing here?'

He shrugged. Nice, broad shoulders, she noticed. Well dressed too, in a beige linen suit and cream turtle-neck, his long, dark hair caught at the nape of his neck in a neat ponytail.

'Same as you, I guess.'

Their eyes met and Susie felt a little frisson of excitement travel up her spine. 'Have you finished?' she asked.

'Sure.'

'I was just going for a coffee – would you like to come along?'

He grinned, clearly appreciating her initiative. 'I know a quiet little place a couple of tube stops away.'

'Lead on, then,' she said, deciding then and there

176

that, if she had her way, coffee was not all she would offer him.

In the event, Shaun was not quite as backward in coming forward as she had expected. After two espressos and a plate of tiny continental cakes, he invited her back to his flat, which happened to be conveniently nearby.

The light of anticipation in his eyes warned her that he wasn't intending to show her his etchings, and Susie made a split second decision.

'Why not?' she said, as if she made such casual arrangements every day of her life.

They walked to the flat, not touching, but each aware of the other, as if an invisible band of electrified energy connected them as they walked along the street. It was the first time Susie had ever gone back to a man's flat with the sole intention of having sex with him and she found the whole idea hugely arousing.

His was the top flat of an old Victorian terrace which had been divided. As he showed her into the high-ceilinged living room, Susie looked around her approvingly. He had decorated it in varying shades of cream and white, even the bare floorboards had been bleached as light as possible. There was a plain glass vase with a small arrangement of bright blue delphiniums on the white-painted coffee table and the sofa was a startling shade of crimson, like a splash of bright, fresh blood in the middle of the room.

'This is very striking,' she said.

'Yes, I like it. Would you like to see the bedroom?'

Their eyes met and Susie sucked in her breath as she saw the heat in his. There was something incredibly erotic about being the object of a man's desire and she found the surge of feminine power an incredible aphrodisiac.

'Why not?' she said for the second time that evening.

He had decorated his bedroom to resemble a monk's cell, or that was what it reminded Susie of. The bare plastered walls were again painted white, the only adornment being a plain wooden cross above the bed. The bed itself was narrow and low, furnished with a single, hard-looking pillow, a white sheet and a thin cream-coloured blanket. A wardrobe against the left-hand wall was made of heavy oak, the doors elaborately carved. It seemed to Susie to be singularly out of place.

Shaun walked across to it now and took something out. Turning back, his eyes shining dully as he faced her, he offered her a pair of handcuffs and a whip.

'Will you use these on me?' he asked.

Susie stared at him, her eyes flicking to the items in his hands in incomprehension. For a second when she had first seen what he had taken out of the wardrobe, she had thought he meant to use them on her and she had felt a margin of fear creep beneath her desire.

As realisation dawned, something else gave an edge to her arousal: a dark, erotic thrill of anticipation that propelled her across the room to take the things from him without further hesitation.

'Get undressed,' she snapped.

He closed his eyes momentarily and swallowed, hard, making his Adam's apple bob in his throat.

'Thank you,' he whispered, then obeyed her with an alacrity which sent another surge of power through Susie's veins.

As she had expected, he had a good body, toned and pumped after hours spent in the gym, the skin coloured gold, stretched taut over muscle and flesh. As he skimmed his trousers down his legs, his unfettered penis swung free, semi-erect, yet not quite sure of itself.

Susie watched him as he stripped off completely, weighing the snub-handled whip in one hand whilst dangling the metal handcuffs from one finger. Once he was naked, Shaun looked expectantly at her, as if awaiting instructions. Susie decided to grasp the nettle.

'On the bed,' she said imperiously, pointing with the blunt end of the whip handle.

Shaun's pupils dilated with pleasure as he obeyed her, lying back so that his head was propped by the pillows, his body straight and submissive.

Playing for time, Susie allowed her eyes to roam contemptuously over his naked flesh.

'You pathetic little worm,' she sneered as her gaze fell on his rising cock. 'This turns you on so much, doesn't it?'

'Yes,' he whispered.

Susie flicked the dangling fronds of the whip across his belly, making him gasp. 'Yes *what*?' she hissed through clenched teeth.

'Yes, mistress,' he said at once. Susie hid a smile. This was too easy. 'That's better. Hands above your head.'

She waited until his arms were stretched above him before leaning forward to clip first one, then the other metal bracelet around his wrists.

Stepping back to admire her handiwork, her eyes took in the taut stretch of the tendons in his shoulders and the slightly pained expression. She smiled cruelly.

'You needn't look like that,' she told him. 'If you think that's uncomfortable, you have a treat in store.'

Stepping forward again, she trailed the ends of the whip across his lips. Instantly, Shaun reached up to kiss the tips, a look of beatific pleasure transforming his features. Eking out the tension, Susie allowed the whip to trail lightly across his chin and down his neck, then she traced a line between his pectorals, over the taut plane of his belly to the now upstanding column of his prick.

'Did I say you could do this?' she said, flicking the whip lightly against the base of his balls.

Shaun gasped and his cock twitched.

'No, mistress,' he choked, his voice trembling with excitement.

'No. I can't let that go unpunished,' she said thoughtfully, touching the whip handle against her lips. 'What am I going to do to you?'

She ran her eyes across his naked body, seeing the need in him, the pearly beads of perspiration pushing through his pores. His cock was standing at right angles to his body now, rigid, as if it had been shot through with a rod of iron. The neat, brown spheres of his nipples had puckered into two hard little promontories, straining towards her, begging to be touched.

Susie understood instinctively how she could prolong his pleasure, make it more intense when it came. She smiled.

Holding his eye, she unclipped the earrings from her ears and moved slowly towards him. He began to breathe in short, shallow little breaths, as if arousal had made him incapable of properly expanding his lungs. Susie perched on the edge of the bed, almost companionably and trailed the tips of her long, plum-painted nails across the very tips of his nipples.

He swallowed, holding his breath as she rolled the cold gold of the earrings over the quivering peaks.

'I don't like clip-on earrings as a rule,' she said conversationally, 'they do *pinch* so. I'm always glad to take them off at the end of the day.'

She pulled back the clip of one earring so that he could see it and allowed it to close again with a viscious snap. Shaun shuddered and Susie laughed.

'It's only what you deserve,' she purred throatily. 'And I *know* it's what you want.'

'Please, mistress . . .' he whispered.

Susie smiled, circling one nipple slowly with a gentle fingertip.

'Please? Do you mean, please don't? Or please do?' As she said the last word, she pulled the nipple between her finger and thumb and snapped one earring into place.

He cried out briefly, but Susie could see by the growing heat in his dark eyes that the small pain she had caused him had been eclipsed by a surge of ecstasy so great she could only wonder at it. His reaction to the second clip was less dramatic but no less appreciated, and she stood back to admire her handiwork.

The thick gold hoops stood proud of his restrained flesh, the gold shining dully against his tan.

'They look rather pretty,' she mused, unbuttoning her blouse as she spoke.

Shaun's eyes widened as she lifted her breasts free from their lacy covering and began to play absently with her own nipples. Brushing her thumbs lightly back and forth, she soon brought them to a hardness which matched his.

'Would you like to touch these?' she asked him.

'Yes, oh yes, mistress,' he said hoarsely, the tendons of his neck straining as he lifted his head to get a better look.

Susie moved towards him again, allowing her breasts to swing free. Shaun's eyes were like saucers, his mouth slack as she leaned over the bed, dangling her breasts within inches of his eager mouth, just out of reach of his outstretched tongue. He groaned as if in pain when she straightened again.

'I don't think so,' she said thoughtfully. 'No, I think I'll warm you up a little first. You'd like that, wouldn't you?'

His eyes met hers and they stared at each other for a few minutes.

'What do you say?' Susie asked, her voice dangerously low.

'I . . . yes please, mistress,' he said miserably.

She smiled and flicked the whip experimentally against the side of her thigh. It made a satisfying *whoosh* as it cut through the air, curling around her leg momentarily as it made contact, not painfully, but with an interesting little sting. Susie imagined how Shaun would feel when it entwined itself around the swollen shaft of his penis and felt her own sex flesh swell in anticipation. She was really rather enjoying herself.

Raising her right arm, she brought the whip down across his thighs.

'Ah!'

It was a sigh rather than a cry of pain, so Susie repeated the manoeuvre slightly above the last stroke, swiftly followed by two more lashes. She was panting slightly now, both with the effort involved and the excitement generated by the power rush which had overwhelmed her at the first stroke. The adrenalin was pumping through her body, making her feel high, and she could feel her clitoris throbbing insistently, taking on a life of its own.

Throwing the whip aside, she hoisted up her skirt and dragged her panties down her legs. They were soaking wet, drenched by the feminine moisture seeping from her sex.

'You're not to come,' she instructed, almost forgetting her role as she straddled him on the bed. 'Do you understand?'

He nodded, clearly not trusting himself to speak. His eyes were wide, their expression glassy as he stared at her. She brought her discarded knickers up to his face and allowed him to breathe in the scent of her. Then she flattened his penis carefully against his belly and began to slide herself up and down the length of him.

The feel of his smooth, silky skin, covering the rigid shaft sent ripples of exquisite pleasure travelling through to her womb. Leaning forward slightly, she angled herself so that her clitoris was receiving direct stimulation as she moved. Beneath her bottom, she could feel the rasp of his hair-roughened thighs against her soft skin, the heat generated by the weals marking his flesh making her burn, intensifying her pleasure.

'Squeeze my tits,' she commanded.

As he moved to obey, Susie experienced the most wonderful rush of euphoria. She had never dreamed how liberating it would be to have a man so wholly at her command, to be able to demand from him whatever she wanted, without thought for his comfort or his ego, and know that she would be instantly obeyed. It was heady stuff, and thinking about the possibilities made her head swim.

For now, though, she wanted only to bring herself to climax. The peak was only seconds away, she could feel the pressure building, the delicious, precious sensation of release already within her grasp.

'Yes,' she whispered, closing her eyes so that all her

concentration could be directed inwards, towards the very core of her.

The man beneath her mattered not at all, he was no more than an object, a masturbatory tool, designed for her pleasure. So long as his cock stayed hard and he continued to knead and pinch her nipples with perfect rhythm, she need not think of him at all.

She came with a shout of pure triumph, a thousand fireworks exploding behind her closed eyelids as her entire body was consumed with wave after wave of undiluted ecstasy. She felt as if she was flying, soaring above her physical body, transcending the mere sex act, entering another dimension.

Then it was over, leaving her feeling exhausted. Opening her eyes, she saw the shame on Shaun's face and knew immediately what had happened. Looking down, she saw the betraying pools of ejaculate spattering his belly and her thighs and her expression hardened.

'I told you not to do that,' she said coldly.

'I'm sorry . . . it was just that you were so lovely . . . I couldn't help it . . . where are you going?' His voice rose on the last, betraying his panic as she wiped herself down with the sheet before dressing.

'I told you not to come,' she repeated flatly.

He sat up. 'Please don't go.'

Susie threw him a contemptuous glance.

'Call me when you think you can exercise more self-control,' she said. Then she walked out, closing the door softly behind her.

Outside, she felt as though she was walking on air. It had been such an exhilarating experience and one which she knew she would want to repeat, when the time was right. Recalling the look on Shaun's face when she left him made her laugh out loud. This was the way she wanted to feel after having sex – a million miles away from how Sebastian had made her feel.

Perhaps she didn't need Sebastian after all? The tantalising thought played around the edges of her mind, offering her a ray of hope in what had become a gloomy situation. She tried to grasp it, to hang on to the sense of optimism, but it was a fleeting respite. Without Sebastian she would have no home, no work, no money.

Reaching into her bag for a handkerchief, her fingers closed over an envelope. Drawing it out, she realised that she'd almost forgotten it was there. The letter had been forwarded to her by the girlie magazine which had carried her photographs. It was from Peter Jones, her father, the first time she'd heard anything of him since he left home. He wrote that he'd seen her picture and wondered if she might be his daughter, Susie. Apparently, he had been reminded of Diana when he saw her. If she was his daughter, he wanted to meet her.

A few short months ago, Susie would have been overjoyed to receive a letter from her father. But then, months before, he wouldn't have seen her naked photograph in a men's magazine. Now she felt too ashamed to see him face to face. Yet if he really wanted to meet her . . . it had taken a great deal of courage for her to ring the number he had sent her that evening. Peter had been polite but distant on the telephone, though they had arranged to meet for dinner. Susie hoped that he would be more approachable in the flesh when she met him that evening than he had sounded on the phone.

She was preoccupied as she stepped out of the lift on the floor where she still shared a flat with Holly, so she didn't see the figure standing by the door until she was almost on top of him.

'Hello, Susie.'

She looked up, startled.

'Adam!'

Her heart seemed to stop beating as she looked up at him and foolish tears stung her eyes, threatening to overflow. She hadn't remembered him being so tall or so good-looking, and she had to admit that seeing him after all these weeks of self-imposed exile was bittersweet.

'What are you doing here?'

'I could ask you the same question. Is this the best your photographer friend could come up with?' He looked around the cold, concrete-walled passageway in distaste.

Susie felt herself bristle. *Same old Adam, immediately rubbing me up the wrong way*, she thought.

'Is that what you've come all this way for – to sneer at where I'm living?'

'No, I came to ask you to send warning the next time I'm likely to find you looking down at me from the top shelf at the newsagents.'

Susie gasped, unprepared for his direct approach.

'I don't want to talk about that,' she mumbled, struggling with her key in the lock of the door.

'Tough. That's what I'm here for.'

'Look, I know it wasn't what I intended to do, but it was all done in good taste. It's not as if there were any really crude pictures, no gynae-shots or anything like that.'

She didn't sound nearly as flip and unconcerned as she clearly hoped, so Adam held his tongue. He watched her fumbling with the key for a few seconds more before, with a muffled exclamation, his hand closed over hers and guided it in.

'Thank you,' she muttered resentfully, pulling her hand abruptly away from the warmth of his. 'You'd better come in, since you're here.'

'You're too kind.'

Inside, Adam's eyes ran around the room, taking in every detail. Suddenly, Susie was acutely conscious of the shabbiness of the flat. Her bedding was in an untidy roll at the end of the couch and neither girl had cleared away the dishes from their takeaway the night before. Susie picked them up now and took them into the kitchen, using the washing-up as an excuse to turn her back on Adam so that he couldn't see her embarrassment.

She could feel his eyes on her as she dispensed with the dishes and put the kettle on. Anything to avoid facing him, having to confront the disgust in his eyes as he looked at her.

Adam watched her clattering the dishes, hostility oozing from every pore. He had been shocked at her appearance when he saw her: she had lost weight and there were worrying shadows and hollows in her face which hadn't been there before.

'What's going on, Susie?' he asked softly after a few minutes.

'What do you mean?'

He walked up behind her and stroked her hair with the tips of his fingers. She flinched as if he had burned her with his touch.

'Come back home with me.'

It wasn't what he had intended to say; the words had simply spilled out unbidden, coming from nowhere, shocking him as much as they shocked her.

'What on earth for?'

She turned to face him. As she realised how close they were to each other, her eyes widened, and she leaned back against the kitchen counter, not daring to touch him, afraid of her own reaction as well as his.

They stared at each other for a few moments. Adam saw that a lot of the innocence had left her eyes and he felt a pang of regret, swiftly followed by fury at Sebastian Semple. Girls like Susie were so trusting, so easy to exploit. Fair game for sharks like Semple.

'Why would I want to come home?' she said, breaking the silence at last.

'Diana misses you,' he replied without hesitation.

'I'll write to her, soon.'

Had he imagined the disappointment that crossed her eyes when he had answered her? He wondered how she might have reacted if he had told the truth, that *he* missed her, far more than he ever thought possible.

'Come home,' was all he could bring himself to say.

Susie regarded him levelly for a long moment. 'I can't come home, not even if I wanted to. I've made a new life for myself here in London, Adam, the kind of life I always dreamed of . . .'

He did no more than raise an eyebrow at her.

'Don't sneer!' she cried. 'I know this place is scruffy, but it's only temporary. Once I start earning I'll be able to afford to rent a place of my own. I've got plenty of work, all arising from that assignment you saw. I know it wasn't in the best possible taste, but sometimes you have to do these things to get your foot on the first rung of the ladder. Sebastian says—'

'Hold up, there – what do you mean: *when you start earning*?' Adam interrupted her, homing in on the most pertinent part of her breathless little speech.

Susie's eyes slid away from his. 'Well, Sebastian has invested a lot of money to get me started, plus, of course, he pays for me to stay here and for my food and clothes. I have to pay him back before I start to earn money in my own right.'

'Susie, how can that be just? Okay, he's entitled to take a cut from your earnings, but he has no right to withhold your money from you. Don't you see? It's a way of keeping you dependent on him.'

'No, Adam, you've got it all wrong! Why can't you trust me to know what's best for me? You're as bad as my mother, assuming that you know best, trying to run my life for me.'

'Dammit, Susie, it's only that we both care about you—' He broke off, realising what he had just admitted to.

Susie looked surprised, but encouragingly pleased. 'Do you? Care about me, I mean?'

'You know I do,' he replied gruffly, unwilling to lay himself on the line. Her face was inches from his, her eyes wide, her lips softly parted. He had only to lean forward slightly and . . .

'Then why can't you be happy for me? You might not approve, but this is what I've always wanted. Please, just leave me alone to live my dream.'

He moved away abruptly, irritated by her wilful naïvety. How could she not see that she was being exploited, and in the most shameful, cynical way?

Taking out a piece of paper and a pen from his jacket pocket, Adam wrote down the name and telephone number of the hotel where he was staying.

'Call me,' he told her, pressing the paper into her hands. 'I'm going to be in London for a few more days and I think we ought to talk some more.'

She shook her head. 'There's nothing to talk about,' she insisted.

'At least let me take you for dinner.'

'I can't, I'm meeting someone tonight. Not like that,' she said when she saw his expression, 'not in the way you imagine. I'm meeting my father.'

Adam's face registered his surprise. 'Really? Did you track him down?'

'No,' she admitted awkwardly, 'as a matter of fact he contacted me after that magazine spread that you saw. So you see, it was lucky, really.'

Adam kept his thoughts to himself. To him, there was something rather suspect about a man who recognised his long-lost daughter on the cover of a men's magazine and then requested a meet.

'That must be very exciting for you,' he said carefully.

'Oh, it is – you can't imagine how good it will be to see him again!'

'Maybe we could meet up tomorrow night then,' he said. 'Meanwhile, give me a call if you should need me, or if you want to talk.'

'Thanks, Adam,' she said, leaning forward to give him a friendly peck on the cheek. 'I will have dinner with you tomorrow, just so long as you promise to try to accept my life choices.'

He grinned.

'Consider it a done deal,' he replied enigmatically.

Susie watched him leave, then glanced down at the address and telephone number he had left her. Carefully, she folded it in half and put it in her handbag.

Chapter Eleven

AS SHE WALKED along the busy early evening streets, looking for the restaurant where she was to meet her father, Susie felt a mixture of excitement and apprehension. What if she didn't recognise him after all these years? What if he didn't recognise her?

She needn't have worried about the latter. As she walked into the little bistro-style coffee shop, a middle-aged man rose from the window table and beckoned her over.

He was shorter than she remembered, and plumper, and his grey hair was lank, styled in a feeble attempt to disguise an incipient bald patch. He was wearing grubby looking, ill-fitting jeans, slung low beneath his paunch, and a light-grey anorak over an off-white shirt, open at the neck to reveal a red, turkey-skin neck that wobbled as he smiled. As she approached, his small, dark eyes darted ceaselessly over her, refusing to make full eye contact.

'Dad?' she said, with a catch in her voice.

'Susie!'

He offered her his hand across the table and she took it awkwardly. His palms were damp, his fingers plump and stubby. They shook hands and both sat down, Susie

191

feeling self-conscious as she surveyed her long-lost parent across the table.

'What would you like to eat?' he asked her.

She recognised his voice at least, and that made her relax a little. 'Lasagne would be good,' she said.

'Drink?'

'A glass of red wine, please.'

To Susie's embarrassment, Peter clicked his fingers at the adolescent employed as waiter, who oozed resentment at such cavalier treatment as he took her order.

'And bring another of these now,' Peter added, passing the boy his empty pint glass, 'and another with the meal.'

They exchanged awkward smiles across the table, but neither seemed to know what to say. If ever she had fantasised about this moment, Susie had never pictured herself lost for words. Now though, sitting opposite this stranger who was her father, she realised that her memories of him had him pickled in aspic, stuck in the past. She had no idea where he had been, how he had been living, even if he had another family somewhere: she didn't know him at all.

'Do you—'

'Does your—'

Both spoke at once and she realised he was probably just as nervous as she. He drank his beer quickly and signalled for another to be brought to the table. Susie caught herself wondering how many he had had before she arrived. He had the ruddy complexion of a seasoned drinker and she noticed that his hands shook as he raised the third glass to his lips.

Their food arrived, saving them from further conversation. Peter tucked in with relish, swilling down each mouthful with beer. When he had finished, he pushed away his plate and issued a loud, unselfconscious belch. He eyed her barely touched lasagne covetously.

'Not hungry?'

Susie shook her head and pushed her plate towards him.

'You have it,' she said.

She watched with fascinated repulsion as he demolished the second plateful. Desperately, she tried to dredge up some feeling, a modicum of affection borrowed from the past, but she could not. All through her childhood she had built up this man into some kind of romantic, mysterious figure who had left her and her mother to fend for themselves, turning his back on the farm and all that came with it for some noble, complex reason. Now all she could see was a man who had abandoned her without a backward glance.

'Why did you never get in touch with us after you left?' she blurted suddenly.

Peter wiped the back of his hand across his lips and signalled for another pint.

'I thought it was best to make a clean break. You know.'

'Not really,' she replied. 'Tell me.'

His eyes narrowed as he looked at her, then he quite literally shrugged off her question.

'I suppose you have to watch what you eat in your line of work,' he said.

Confused for a moment by the total change of subject, Susie was silent.

'I mean, a whole lasagne would *show* wouldn't it, if you were stripping off tomorrow?' He chuckled.

Susie felt herself bridle.

'That isn't normally what I do,' she told him stiffly. 'I came to London to be a fashion model.'

'Course you did. It gave your old dad quite a thrill to see you in that magazine, I can tell you. I showed it around at the hostel – gave me a bit of . . . what do you call it these days? Street cred.'

Susie suppressed a shudder at the mental picture she had of her father showing around the compromising pictures of her. It didn't strike her as being a very fatherly thing to do.

'You live in a hostel?' she asked him.

He waved a hand airily.

'Just temporary. I expect you're earning a bob or two now, aren't you?'

'Not really,' Susie replied, alarm bells clanging in her head.

'Oh, come on, you can tell me! Taking your clothes off pays well, doesn't it?'

His eyes were round and hot as he looked at her and Susie felt her flesh creep. She didn't want to know what he was implying, though sadly she could guess.

'Why exactly *did* you get in touch with me?' she asked him abruptly.

Peter sat back in his chair and drained his glass before answering her.

'It's good to see you, Susie. After all, it's been a long time.'

She wasn't fooled.

'And?'

He shrugged, not even bothering to try to pretend now.

'Things have been hard for me, these past few years. The recession still hasn't completely gone away for most of us, you know. All I need to get back on my feet is for someone to put a bit of faith in me, give me a stake, if you like.'

Susie felt something harden in the centre of her chest. 'You want *me* to give you *money*?'

'Not much, just enough to get me back in business. And after all, we are family, aren't we?'

Susie stared at him, barely able to contain her fury. To think that she had wanted to meet this man, had thought of him fondly all these years! And now all he wanted was her non-existent money. If only he knew!

'Excuse me,' she said sweetly, 'I need to visit the little girls' room.'

Peter raised his glass at her, confident that he had found a new source of beer money. As he began his next pint, he didn't notice Susie walk straight past the toilets and out into the street.

'Baby! What's wrong?'

Susie began to cry the minute she walked through the door of the flat. Haltingly, she told Holly the whole sorry story.

'The sleaze!' her friend exclaimed as she came to the part about the money. 'His own daughter, too!'

Susie laid her head on her friend's shoulder and allowed herself to relax in her embrace. Holly was stroking her hair comfortingly. She felt incredibly weary after her encounter with her father and now, more than at any other time, she missed Diana. Thinking of the things she had said to her about driving her father away . . . now she had met Peter she could guess at the truth, and she felt thoroughly ashamed.

Adam was right, she shouldn't have left it so long before calling her mother. She sighed. She seemed to have got so many things wrong.

'That was a big sigh, Susie,' Holly said softly. 'Want to tell me about it?'

Susie closed her eyes, soothed by the rhythmic stroking of her forehead.

'I don't know, Holly. I sometimes wonder if I've done the right thing, coming here. Maybe I haven't got what it takes after all.'

Holly's fingers stilled for a second, then she began to move them in slow, soothing strokes across the top of Susie's scalp.

'Mmm, that's nice,' Susie said.

'So what did you expect – that you'd be a star overnight?' Holly teased her gently.

That's what Sebastian implied, Susie thought. Aloud, she said, 'Maybe. I don't know. Let's face it, a couple of lingerie ads and a spread in a men's magazine doesn't amount to much in nearly three months, does it?'

Holly leaned forward and kissed her gently on the top of the head. 'These things take time,' she soothed.

'But how much time? How long have you been waiting for your big break, Holly? Well?'

'A while,' the other girl admitted.

'You see! And you're *gorgeous*. What hope do I have if you haven't been noticed yet?'

Holly chuckled softly. 'You know the right things to say, girlfriend!' she said wryly.

'No, I mean it,' Susie countered earnestly, sitting up so that they were facing each other. 'You're the loveliest girl I've ever seen outside the pages of a magazine. So what do I have to do to get noticed?'

Holly looked thoughtfully at her for a moment. Then: 'You have to do what Sebastian tells you to do.'

Susie sat back, exasperated.

'He just keeps telling me to hang in there until something comes up.'

'And it will – be patient.'

She leaned forward and pressed her lips against Susie's, kissing her full on the mouth. It was the first time they had kissed since the party and stunned, Susie did not react, except to open her eyes wider. It wasn't the same in the cold light of day. Holly's lips were soft and moist, her small teeth sharp as they nipped gently at the tender flesh of Susie's lower lip. Susie stiffened involuntarily as she ran the tip of her tongue lightly along the inner edge. Pulling back, Holly gave her a small, secret smile and went to make them both a drink.

The following afternoon, Susie was woken at noon by Holly softly calling her name.

'What is it?' she asked sleepily.

'Sebastian wants us at the flat – he has work for us,' the other girl told her.

Dragging herself out of bed, Susie showered and dressed, not bothering with make-up until she knew what was required.

'Come on – don't dawdle!' Holly urged her as they left the flat, her spike-heeled boots clicking along the pavement.

Not for the first time, Susie felt resentful that, after days of waiting around with little to do, Sebastian simply clicked his fingers and they were expected to rush halfway across London at his whim. She wanted to spend all day in bed, then party all night, not argue with Sebastian about how much more she was prepared to reveal of herself for the next assignment. She was tired and the meeting with her father had left her feeling depressed. And then there was Adam.

Knowing he was in London, expecting to see her again made Susie feel unsettled, with mixed emotions. The sight of him, after weeks of trying to forget the kiss they had shared, had stirred up all the confusing, conflicting emotions that she had managed to put aside when she left.

'You're not still thinking about your daddy, are you?' Holly said, breaking into her reverie as they sat back in a cab.

'No, I was just thinking of . . . of somebody at home.'

Holly gave her an odd look and frowned. 'Best keep your mind on your work today – Sebastian will expect you to concentrate.'

'Of course. Any idea what this job's about?'

'He didn't say.' Holly looked out of the window, not wanting to catch Susie's eye.

She'd noticed before that Holly often seemed cagey when it came to talking about Sebastian. She supposed it was natural, considering the relationship she had with him, but there seemed to be more to it than that. It made her feel uneasy now as they drew up outside the tower block and paid off the cab driver.

Sebastian greeted them both effusively and ushered them through to the living room. As before, the stage was set ready for the shots he wanted to produce, but this time Holly did not merely chaperone Susie to the flat, she stayed and took off her coat.

'There's some champagne on ice in the kitchen,' Sebastian told her, never taking his eyes off Susie. 'Why don't you pour us all a glass before we start?'

'Are we celebrating something?' Susie asked, happy that he appeared to be in a good mood. He could be difficult if he wasn't in a reasonable humour, but when he turned on the charm she still enjoyed his company.

'That depends on you, sweetheart,' he replied enig-matically as he took her coat and they sat down.

Holly came in with the champagne and Sebastian poured them all a glass.

'To collaboration,' he said, raising his glass in a toast.

Susie sipped her champagne cautiously. The other two seemed wired, as if nervous about something, and she had the uncomfortable impression that their agitation stemmed from her. Looking round the room, she saw that there was a trio of video recorders set up on tripods around the makeshift podium, which today was draped in turquoise velvet. A worm of suspicion crept under her skin.

'What's going on?' she asked, putting down her glass.

'We're going to make a little movie,' Sebastian told her, watching her face closely, as if expecting some kind of reaction.

'What kind of movie?'

'The kind that a beautiful girl like you is perfect for. Holly's going to be in it with you, so you don't need to be nervous.'

'I . . . I don't think—'

'That's right, Susie – you don't need to think. Let Holly show you what to do, and together we'll make you a star.'

Sebastian had costumes ready for them in the small dining room leading off from the living room. Susie eyed her plain black tunic and white blouse dubiously.

'It looks like a uniform,' she whispered to Holly.

'It's a gym-slip. Wise up, girl, and get yourself into gear.' Holly wiggled her way into a tight-fitting grey pencil skirt and a severe looking blue blouse which buttoned up to her throat. Apparently oblivious to Susie's scrutiny, she twisted her hair up into a coil on the top of her head and donned wire-rimmed spectacles.

199

'You're not dressed,' she stated flatly when she turned round and saw Susie looking at her.

'No. I don't want to do this.'

'You didn't want to be photographed with your blouse off,' Sebastian said from the doorway, 'but once you started it was fine. You were a natural. It'll be the same with this. Trust me.'

Susie stared at him and knew that she did not trust him one little bit.

'I'm sorry, but I'm not prepared to make a film. Not any kind of film. I want to be a model.'

'And so you shall be,' Sebastian soothed, putting his arm around her shoulder and easing her into the living room. 'Lots of models go into the movies. Elle Macpherson, Lauren Hutton . . .'

'That was *after* they made their names as models,' Susie pointed out.

This seemed to try Sebastian's patience one step too far. 'Just get into costume and haul yourself on the stage.'

Susie recognised that cold, implacable tone from when he had taken the nude photographs of her. This time, something within her rebelled and she stood her ground.

'No,' she said, her voice small but firm, 'I don't want to do it. I'm sorry.'

'Sorry? There's money in this, Susie, for *all* of us. Don't start being awkward now.'

'Yeah, and I need the money,' Holly said sourly.

Susie looked from one to the other of them, realising she was seeing them clearly for the very first time. Her so-called friend and the man who had promised her mother he would look after her. Neither of them cared about her at all. She was no more than a pawn in a game. It was as if a curtain had been tweaked aside so that at last she could see clearly what was on the other side. She didn't like what she saw.

'I'm not so naïve that you can take advantage of me like this,' she said, unable to stop her voice from quivering as she faced them.

'Take advantage of you? Oh, come on, don't be silly! I'm helping you to get what you want, Susie. Never forget that.'

Susie went over to the pile of blank film cassettes Sebastian had ready by the first camera.

'*Older Woman Teaches Lesbian Virgin All She Knows*,' she read aloud. 'I suppose this is art too?'

'In its way. Grow up, Susie – you're in the real world now. You've hung on to your rose-tinted spectacles for far too long already. It's time you faced up to what you are.'

'Which is?' she queried quietly.

He didn't need to answer, Susie could see what he thought of her in his eyes. And at that moment she hated him for stringing her along, for trying to do this to her. Though her legs were shaking and her heart was banging so hard she could feel it in her ears, Susie stood her ground.

'I might well have been naïve, but this isn't what I left home for,' she said, 'and I'm not doing it.'

She retrieved her coat and made for the door.

'If you go through that door, your modelling career will be finished,' Sebastian said furiously.

'I don't care. If you think I still owe you any money, then send a bill to my home address. But just for the record, I think you're wrong. I *have* got what it takes – *you* just don't know how to handle it.'

She walked out, slamming the door behind her. She

201

half expected Sebastian, or even Holly, to come after her, but to her relief she made it out through the main doors unmolested. She felt as if a great weight had been lifted from her shoulders, only to be replaced by another, equally pressing. What on earth would she do now?

Alongside the apprehension, though, she was conscious of a huge surge of adrenalin pumping through her veins, looking for an outlet. She was buzzing with it and the thrill of what she had just done excited her, turning her on in a way she had never experienced before.

Hailing a passing taxi, she sat back in the seat and thought of Shaun. If she went to his flat now she was in the mood to give him the time of his life. She grimaced. Shaun was no challenge – she needed more.

Then she remembered what Adam had said about hanging around for a while. A dull, rhythmic pulse began to beat in the innermost recesses of her feminine heart. Closing her eyes, she pictured Adam bound and helpless, herself wielding absolute power over him, and the dull pulse grew stronger, faster, so that she almost came there and then.

Leaning forward, she gave the driver the address of his hotel.

Chapter Twelve

HE OPENED THE door to his hotel room dressed in nothing more than a small, white towel.

'Susie?'

His face registered surprise at seeing her, his pleasure guarded, but obvious in the dilating pupils of his eyes. Susie smiled knowingly, casting her own eyes over him briefly, from head to toe, drinking him in.

His dark hair was wet, moulding his scalp and curling on to his wide shoulders. The broad sweep of his well-defined chest glistened with droplets of water. Where it had been exposed to the sun, his skin was the colour of fudge, covered by a sprinkling of fine, dark hair.

'You said I could call on you.'

Her voice sounded low and husky, alien to her own ears. She watched as Adam's eyes darkened, the pupils expanding still more until there was no more than a thin, gold-brown rim of the iris showing.

'Of course. Is there something wrong?'

She didn't answer him, merely feasting her eyes on the naked expanse of his skin, breathing in the clean, masculine scent of him until it made her head spin.

'I'll go and get dressed—'

'No!' She put out her hand to stop him. A jolt of

electricity shot up her arm from her fingertips, making her catch her breath. 'Don't go.'

Holding his eye, she reached out and slipped the tip of her forefinger beneath the upper edge of the towel. Running it slowly along the waistline, she felt the heat of his rising cock through the soft fabric and knew she had what she wanted.

'Susie . . . ?'

Adam's own voice was gratifyingly gruff. His body was taut, tension emanating from every pore as he waited to see what she would do next. A small pulse beat in his clenched jaw as he stared at her. Holding his eye, she reached up to press her lips against it.

Adam swallowed and moved away. 'Don't play games with me, Susie,' he warned her.

She smiled, supremely confident. 'You don't like games?' she queried softly. 'Won't you play with me, Adam?'

She pulled the towel away from his body and dropped it on the floor at their feet. Adam shivered as her cool hands enclosed his erection and Susie felt a rush of feminine power. That she could give him pleasure so simply seemed to her to be a wondrous thing.

His cock was like a rod of steel encased in fine velvet. Imagining it easing its way inside her brought her out in goosebumps. But that was for later; there were other things she wanted to do with him first.

'Aren't you going to invite me in?'

Adam started, as if he had completely forgotten that they were still standing in the open doorway of his hotel room. Stepping back, he raised his eyebrows as Susie followed him, her fist closing more firmly around his cock. She smiled at him and kicked the door closed behind them. Without loosening her grip, she led him through to the bedroom and guided him towards a chair.

'Sit,' she said with soft command.

Adam sat, his eyes following her as she moved around the room, trailing her fingers along the tops of the furniture, familiarising herself with the place.

It was a standard, modern hotel room; square and sparsely furnished with a bed, a chair, a small wardrobe and a dressing table with an over-large mirror making it look top-heavy. The curtains at the window were an uninspiring dusky pink, the carpet grey and worn in places. It would do for what she had in mind.

At the window, she unhooked the tasselled rope tie-backs and drew the curtains, shutting out the daylight and plunging the room into a gloomy half-light. Draping the tie-backs across her arm, she turned on the lamp which sat on the dressing table and opened a drawer. Inside, she found a belt and tie. Her heart began to beat a little faster. Would she really get away with this – with *Adam*?

Turning towards him, she smiled when she saw the wariness in his eyes.

'You've wanted me for a long time, Adam, haven't you?' she asked him conversationally.

'What?'

'It's all right. I've wanted you too. Only, I never really understood *how* I wanted you, if you know what I mean.'

'Susie . . .'

'Shut up.'

Adam looked shocked, but he let her continue without any further attempt at interruption.

'If you want me, Adam, you've got to play a game with me first. Nod once if you agree that you'll play, darling.'

Though she noticed that he gritted his teeth as he did it, Adam dipped his head in response. Susie moved behind him, allowing her lips to brush his hair.

'I'm so glad you did that,' she murmured.

Adam let out his breath on a sigh as she ran her hands down his arms in a sensuous caress. She loved the feel of soft skin over iron-hard muscle, the silky hair on his forearms tickling her fingertips as she stroked.

'I've always loved your hands,' she mused aloud as their fingers intertwined. 'They're so strong . . . so capable, yet so sensitive . . . the times I've fantasised about them moving across my naked skin . . .'

Allowing her fingers to slip from between his, she circled his wrists with her thumb and middle finger, measuring the gap between them.

'Do you trust me, darling?' she asked him, nuzzling into the warm hollow behind his ear.

'Not for a minute,' he replied, his voice thick with desire.

Susie chuckled.

'Oh, good!' she said, bringing his wrists together behind his back. 'That makes things so much more *interesting*, don't you think?'

She wrapped one of the tie-backs in a figure-of-eight around his wrists and tied it firmly in a knot. Eyeing her handiwork dubiously, she reckoned that with one determined tug he could probably shrug off the bondage and be free, but instinct told her he was unlikely to do so. Though he was wary of her at the moment, she could tell by the tension apparent in every line of his body that she was turning him on and that he wasn't likely to do anything to jeopardise the eventual outcome.

'Comfortable?' she purred in his ear.

Adam did not reply, though he shivered convulsively

as she licked delicately at the whorl of his ear, breathing softly into it.

Picking up the tie, Susie wrapped it around his eyes and knotted it firmly at the back of his head. It wasn't wide enough to completely blindfold him but it was sufficient to restrict his vision so that he could experience the thrill of being totally at her mercy.

Moving away from him, Susie perched on the edge of the double bed which dominated the room and stretched luxuriously.

'Mmm. You do look wonderful like that. Better than my wildest imaginings. You see, I had such *romantic* ideas about sex before I'd experienced it. All that love and goo-goo eyes stuff . . . I actually thought that was what sex was for!' She laughed lightly. 'Now I know different. And I'm glad we didn't get together when I was that naïve. Because now I know what to do with you, Adam Corcoran, it's going to be so much fun for both of us!'

Adam did not say a word, but his body betrayed his arousal. Moving towards him, Susie kissed the corner of his mouth so lightly it made his lips tremble as he sucked in his breath. She walked her fingertips down his neck and along each collarbone in turn. Running her forefinger lightly between his pectorals, she circled his nipples, scratching gently at the hard little buttons of flesh. Smoothing the still-damp skin over his shoulders, she dipped her head to lick down his midline to his navel.

The velvety tip of his penis brushed the end of her chin in an involuntary caress which made the air hiss between his teeth as he tried to cage a cry.

'Naughty!' she admonished him. 'We need to put this away for now.'

She tapped her finger sharply against his cock, making him jump. Reaching under her skirt, she unclipped her stockings from their suspenders and rolled them down her legs.

From the way Adam cocked his head, she knew he was listening intently, trying to work out what she was doing. She smiled to herself, allowing her fingers to play briefly against the damp gusset of her panties, keeping herself on the edge.

'Don't you come now, Adam, or it'll all be over. You wouldn't want it to be over just yet, would you, darling?'

'No,' he replied in a hoarse whisper.

'Sit still, then,' she told him as she made ropes of the fine nylon stockings.

Kneeling in front of him, she wound one stocking around his swollen shaft, criss-crossing it from tip to stem, then passing it once beneath his testicles like a sling. Taking the second stocking, she bound his wrapped penis flat against his belly, tying it firmly around his waist and securing it at the back.

'There,' she said with satisfaction. 'Try getting out of that!'

'Susie . . .'

'Ssh!' She kissed him softly on the lips. 'You can trust me really, you know,' she murmured against his mouth, breathing in his warm, sweet breath. 'Would you like to be able to see now?'

He nodded and she reached up to untie the blindfold. He blinked several times while his eyes adjusted. Looking down at his bound cock, he grimaced, making her laugh softly.

'It's not for long,' she promised, 'and it'll be worth it in the end . . . You'll see.'

She kissed him again, enjoying the sensation of warm, moist flesh sliding against her own, allowing the waves of fresh arousal to pass over her, bathing her in a warm, thrilling glow.

Reluctantly, she moved away from him and went to stand by the bed where he could see her. Holding his eye, she began to undress.

She was wearing a long, button-through dress in dark red cotton voile which swung sensuously around her bare calves as she walked. Her feet were encased in flimsy red high-heeled sandals, held on to her foot by a single strap over the toes and one around her heel.

Her hair had grown a little since her visit to the hairdresser and for the assignment with Sebastian she had pinned it up on top of her head in a careless knot. Now, watching Adam watching her, she began to remove the pins one by one, flicking them away from her and allowing her thick blond hair to fall messily around her face.

When all the pins had been removed, she ran her fingers through her hair, pushing it back off her face and shaking it out of her eyes. Slowly she began to unbutton her dress. Adam groaned and closed his eyes. She saw his Adam's apple bob in his throat as he swallowed and his cock swelled against its bonds making them tighter.

'Open your eyes,' she directed, her voice soft but with an implacable note of command which brooked no argument.

She waited until he was focusing on her again before continuing, her fingers working deftly to unfasten the tiny buttons so that her dress fell apart, settling either side of her breasts. Slowly, relishing Adam's enjoyment, she pushed the dress on to her shoulders and allowed it to fall softly down her arms and into a silky heap on the floor.

Standing in the muted glow of the side lamp, she let him drink in the sight of her for a few minutes. She was wearing a white bra and pants set in a shiny, transparent material which left nothing to the imagination. The panties had suspenders attached which dangled uselessly now against the creamy skin at the tops of her thighs, providing a frame for the dark triangle of her pubis. Susie knew that there was a damp, spreading stain of moisture at the front of the panties which Adam could see from where he sat.

Deciding to keep on her shoes, she reached behind her back to unclip her bra. Her breasts fell softly into her waiting hands, eliciting another low moan from Adam.

'Do you like these?' she asked him rhetorically. 'Imagine slipping that lovely cock between them . . .' She pressed the sides of her breasts together to create a channel and leaned forward slightly from the waist to give him a better view. 'You could slide back and forth, back and forth, and then—'

'Susie . . . please . . .' he cried, 'no more!'

She laughed.

'No more? Oh, darling – where's your stamina?'

His eyes widened as she slipped her hand inside her panties and stroked the swollen folds of her sex.

'Mmm, these are so wet, I'm going to have to take them off.'

She skimmed the panties down her legs and waved them at him. 'Perfume,' she said, 'the sweetest perfume of all. If only they could bottle this . . .' She threw them aside and slipped her fingers between her legs again.

'God, I am *so* wet. Can you see?'

She eased her bottom back on the bed and allowed her legs to slide apart. Adam's eyes fell on to the soft, moist folds of her sex and his cock began to throb visibly.

'Easy,' she cautioned, stroking lazily along the channels either side of her labia. 'You can't come like that and if it swells much more my stockings will cut into your flesh.'

He was breathing shallowly, straining forward in his seat as her fingers found the swelling nub of her clitoris and began to circle it. Round and round in ever-decreasing circles.

'Oh, that's good ... so good ...' she whispered, bringing her knees up so that the soles of her sandals were flat against the bedcover. Opening her legs wider, she peeled away the moist leaves of flesh with the first two fingers of her left hand while with the middle finger of her right she brought up the moisture from the entrance to her body and bathed her clitoris with it.

'Untie me, Susie,' Adam begged, scraping the chair closer to the bed.

'Stay where you are!' she gasped, circling faster now as the warmth seeped through her, radiating out from her belly and suffusing her limbs.

He stayed, watching helpless as her climax began to build, spiralling out of control. A rosy flush spread across her chest and up her neck and her mouth ran dry as she neared the peak. Holding his eye, she circled her lips with the tip of her tongue in a vain attempt to moisten them. She began to tap her fingerpad rhythmically against the throbbing protuberance, beating a response from it that made her rear up from the bed, scissoring her legs in the air as her orgasm broke.

'Ah! Oh, God ... yes!'

All the breath seemed to leave her in a whoosh as she fell back against the pillows, spent. It was several minutes before she began to come back down to earth. Gradually she became aware of the tense silence surrounding her, the only sound Adam's harsh, laboured breathing.

Opening her eyes, she saw that his jaw was set with the effort of holding back his own climax. His cock was swollen, pushing through the gaps in its bondage and his entire body was filmed with a fine sheen of perspiration. She smiled happily at him.

'Poor Adam,' she purred, moving lazily to his side.

Dropping to her knees, she touched her fingers against his tortured shaft. He winced and she made a sympathetic noise at the back of her throat. Dipping her head, she soothed the reddened flesh with her tongue while with her hands she quickly untied the bonds.

He gasped as the pressure was released and she unwound the stockings from his penis. At once the blood surged along the stem, quite painfully, judging by Adam's muffled exclamation.

'You poor thing!' Susie cried. Afraid that she might have bound him too tightly, or left him for too long, she slipped his cock into her mouth and suckled on it, bathing it in her saliva and licking at the marks the stockings had left.

'Jeez! Susie . . . I can't hold out . . .'

She raised her head for long enough to look him in the eye and say, 'then don't.'

Adam pulled his hands out of the bondage and ran his fingers through her hair, holding her head as she fellated him. He knew he couldn't hold out for much longer, but he wanted to prolong this moment of delicious agony for as long as possible.

This wasn't what he had expected when he had fantasised about being with Susie. He had thought that she would be sweet and loving, but basically submissive. He had thought he would have to teach her, to coax her slowly along the path of sensuality as she turned from a girl into a woman. He hadn't expected her to be as confident and exciting as this.

With a huge effort of will, he eased her head off him and, taking control, lifted her by the elbows so that she was sitting astride him. He could feel the hot, soft flesh of her sex spread over his thigh as he pulled her closer, the tip of his cock homing in on the open gateway of her cunt.

As she sank down on him, he drew her face down to his and kissed her, thrusting his tongue into her mouth in time with his cock as it burrowed deeper into her.

They sat, entwined, for several minutes, staring mutely at each other, as if assimilating the power of what was happening to them. He couldn't wait any longer. With a muffled groan, he rose to his feet and carried her, her legs gripping his waist, her arms around his neck and her sex sucking at his, the short distance to the bed. With back-breaking control, he lowered her so that her bottom was on the very edge, her legs dangling down so that he could kneel on the floor between her thighs.

From this angle he could penetrate as deeply as the human body would allow. Now he began to move, thrusting in and out of her with increasing speed and ferocity so that she cried out, a second orgasm triggered by the friction of his body moving inside hers.

As the spasms made her vaginal muscles contract, Adam felt the ejaculate being squeezed along his shaft, as if she were milking him. He came with a shout of pure masculine energy, spurt after spurt of hot, viscous semen hitting the neck of her womb, making her his.

He felt triumphant, nine feet tall, on top of the world, as if he could shout from the rooftops, if only he had the energy. As it was, it was all he could do to pull her into his arms and cover them both with the top sheet before they fell into a satisfied slumber.

'Hold me, Adam,' she whispered.

His hands were gentle as they moved across her back and arms, stroking, smoothing, caressing, re-stoking the flames of desire which smouldered dormant within her. Susie ran her toes along the outside of his calf, revelling in the scrape of his coarser body hair against her tender skin.

He broke away from her mouth to kiss a delicate path of small, sucking kisses down the side of her neck, dipping his tongue lightly in the hollow where her collarbones met, making her shiver. His hands cupped her breasts, the thumbs passing lightly over her nipples which leapt to eager attention, puckering and hardening into two needy little peaks.

She moaned as his lips closed over one. As he sucked and licked at her nipple, she felt an answering tug deep in her womb and knew that her sex had grown heavy and moist once more between her tightly closed thighs. After the first crazy, exciting time, Susie was content to simply let him love her this time.

As if reading her mind, Adam stroked the soft swell of her belly, his fingertips lightly brushing the edge of her pubic hair, making her toes curl with anticipation. His head dipped lower. His tongue circled the ridge of her navel, dipping lightly inside before edging further down, towards the protected mound of her sex.

She gasped, holding her breath as the tip of his tongue delved confidently into the cleft of her labia, brushing tantalisingly close to her clitoris. Gently, he manoeuvred her so that she was lying flat on her back. Easing her thighs apart slightly, he marked a trail of small, open-mouthed kisses on the soft flesh of her inner thighs.

As soon as his lips closed over the tiny bud of her clitoris, Susie knew she was lost. Little waves of ecstasy broke over her, making her shake. When he licked boldly along the crease of her labia, she felt the moist sex flesh quiver against his tongue, vibrating as if with a life of its own.

Reaching down, she tangled her fingers in his hair and pressed his face gently against the mound of her sex. He nuzzled at the swollen folds, flicking his tongue lightly across the shiny surface of her clitoris, sending little sparks of sheer ecstasy through her tender flesh. An incredible warmth spread through her, suffusing her with a gentle, golden light.

'Oh, Adam . . .' she whispered as the tiny button began to pulse and the gold splintered in her mind's eye into a myriad of rainbow-coloured pieces.

He pressed the flat of his tongue against it, as if wanting to feel every quiver, each glorious spasm as she came. Her orgasm broke over her in waves, rolling through her torso and spreading into her limbs with a lazy golden glow, lighting her from within.

When he raised his head, her face was full of wonder.

'I had no idea it could be like that,' she whispered, parting her legs instinctively and lifting them up to wrap them round his waist.

With a smile so full of love it brought tears to her eyes, Adam sank slowly into her. Once he was fully inside her, he lay very still for a few minutes, his hands framing her head tenderly, gazing into her eyes.

'Susie . . .' he whispered, his voice catching on her name.

'I love you,' she said. She had no idea where it came from but knew there was nothing else she could say which would even begin to capture the way she felt at that moment.

Adam smiled, silently echoing her words as he kissed her, moving his mouth gently back and forth across her lips. Then he seemed to shiver and the spasm quivered through him, transmitting itself to her.

Susie sucked in her breath, holding him close to her as he began to move inside her. She felt the sensations feathering along the inside of her sex, making her womb contract and her clitoris pulse anew. Then she was falling . . . falling . . .

Reason slipped away to be replaced by the most incredible, all-encompassing sensation she had ever experienced.

They rolled together on the bed so that she was on top of him, able to see his face. His eyes were half closed, his jaw clenched as he reached the peak. As he came, the tendons in his neck stood out and he sighed raggedly. Susie thought it was the sweetest sound she had ever heard, and leaned over him impulsively so that she could kiss him.

As she did so, she inadvertently angled herself so that the vibrations of his orgasm triggered an answering response, deep in her vagina. Taken by surprise, her eyes opened wide and she cried out, falling across him as wave after wave of intense pleasure washed over her.

216

And for one glorious, memorable moment, they were one, joined together by a joy which transcended the physical, taking them to a place to which only love has the key.

Adam held her as she drifted contentedly, snuggled against his chest. She had told him about her father and the video that Sebastian and Holly had planned to make with her. As he stroked her hair, he reflected on how much she had matured since she had left home. He would never have thought that the Susie Jones he first met could have dealt with the situation in which she had found herself yesterday. Quite apart from the way she had so determinedly seduced him mere hours before . . .

She stirred and he smiled down at her.

'You okay?'

She nodded and smiled happily.

'I've never been okay-er.'

'So – what now? Are you planning to come home with me tomorrow?'

A shadow passed across her face as she confronted the death of all her dreams.

'I suppose so.'

'It doesn't have to be forever. Come for a break, then we could come back to London and see about you trying out for a real modelling agency.'

The light reappeared in Susie's eyes.

'You'd come with me?'

'Sure. Now I've found you, you needn't think I'm ever going to let you slip away from me again!'

They kissed; a long, loving, satisfying kiss. When they broke apart, Susie stared down at him, her expression suddenly serious.

'We'd be partners,' she said, 'equal footing.'

'Sure. Perfect partners.'

A mischievous glint came into her eye.

'But how can we be sure we'd be compatible?' she said.

He pretended to consider.

'I guess we'll just have to keep testing,' he replied.

'Mmm – sounds good to me,' she agreed, sliding her hand sensuously along the inside of his thigh. 'How rigorous do you think these tests should be?'

'Oh, very rigorous,' he said, catching his breath as she enclosed his hardening penis in her fist. 'Real . . . extensive.'

'Then we'd better not waste any time, had we?' she said, sliding slowly under the covers.

Adam did not reply.